Sundancer's Star

A Heartwarming Romance

Elsie Davis

Sweet Romance Publishing

Cover Design by getcovers.com

Edited by Elaine Hyatt (Clarity Editing Services) & Cassandra Cornell

Sweet Romance Publishing

Sweetromancepublishing.com

PO Box 778

Liberty, NC 27298

Isaiah 40:31

"But those who hope in the Lord will renew their strength. They will soar on wings like eagles; they will run and not grow weary, they will walk and not be faint."

Contents

Chapter One

♥

The sun was warm as it peeked through the billowing white clouds that drifted across the sky. Children laughed and played at Sugarcreek Park, racing between the playground equipment in search of fun. The sidewalks were laid out in a figure-eight pattern, giving easy access to all the grassy areas and both parking lots at either end of the park. Couples had spread blankets out to picnic near the pond or by the pink and white flowering azalea bushes, lost in their own world of love. The sight always managed to make Caleb's heart ache as memories of times with his wife filled him with grief. Times he couldn't get back with Lauren buried in Dover's cemetery.

Caleb continually kept watch over the visitors coming and going from the park. One couldn't be too careful in protecting your children. The small town was safe enough, but parenting came with a huge set of responsibilities. One of which was keeping their kids out of the emergency room, or any other number of worse scenarios possible.

Accidents happened and in a split second, life could change for the worse. A worse Caleb knew all too well after seeing his wife thrown from a horse. Lauren's final request was for his promise to love and protect their daughter, and then the love of his life had died in his arms. Carrying her body back to town had been the longest horseback ride of his life.

And the last.

Eighteen months had passed since that horrific day. Time in which Caleb found himself immersed in learning how to be a single parent to his young daughter and failing miserably in the beginning. Joelle was full of life and always looking for adventure, a trait she got from her mother. The difficulty came in setting up parameters to protect her, and yet still let her be a child and have fun. His rules might not win him any father-of-the-year points, but they would keep his daughter out of harm's way, at least to the best of his abilities.

"Push me higher, Daddy," Joelle called out. His daughter's vocabulary and ability to communicate was well beyond her age, but then having your father as your constant companion would have that effect. Caleb had the option of sending her to pre-school last year but chose to keep her at home. Whether for her sake or his, he wasn't sure. Maybe a little bit of both. Unfortunately, with Joelle's unexpected maturity came another trait Caleb wasn't fond of in the least. Joelle had grown fearless...something that left him reeling as he tried to control his daughter's thrill to push the limits.

"You're already going plenty high enough on the swing," Caleb said, giving the seat another small push forward.

"No, it's not. I want to go higher like the other kids," Joelle whined, twisting in the seat to look at him, a frown marring her pixie face.

"We've had this discussion before. We do this my way, or we go home. No complaining. Daddy loves you and it's my job to keep you safe." Caleb's heart pounded in his chest as he pictured the image of Joelle coming out of the swing and catapulting toward the ground. It was the what-if scenarios that played out in his head that dictated what his daughter could do and couldn't do. Yes, to the merry-go-round...if they went slow. No, to the teeter totter...ever. There was nothing safe about bouncing up and down with no restraints. Yes, to the slides...if he was close at hand.

Joelle was his everything in life now that he had lost Lauren, and his tolerance for anything dangerous was low.

As in zero.

"I'm safe, Daddy. I'm a big girl now. I'm almost six," she said, obviously unwilling to accept his decision at face value.

The sky darkened and Caleb was surprised to discover ominous clouds had rolled in, fully blotting out the sun. This morning they had grocery shopping and playtime at the park on the to-do list, but now, by the looks of things, they might have to go to Plan B. The rain-out plan.

"Almost five and half is more like it, and that's pushing it. How about we discuss this later, because right now, it looks like a storm is coming. We should get home, so we don't get caught in the rain." This morning the sky had promised a beautiful day and Caleb had skipped checking the weather report. A mistake he vowed not to make again.

"But I want to stay and play. It's not raining yet." Her whining was reaching a level that would soon result in tears.

Caleb stopped the swing and unhooked the harness while holding Joelle in place with the other hand. "If we go now, we won't get wet and then I don't have to worry about you catching a cold."

His daughter slid out of the red seat, using the rope to stay upright. "There's nothing to do at home and I want to stay here." Hands on hips, her pouty face turned upward, Joelle was determined to have her way.

"There's lots to do. We can play games, draw, paint, color, read, or watch a movie," he said as they started down the sidewalk that led to the parking lot.

"We always do those things."

They were creative activities that suited both fun and learning, and they were items that would remain on their to-do list until Joelle went to kindergarten this fall. That is, if Caleb didn't decide to home school his daughter. Letting her venture out away from home and without him scared the dickens out of him. Full-time parenting for Caleb had been anything but successful in the early months. Between dealing with his grief and learning Joelle's routines and needs, there simply hadn't been enough time in a day to do everything.

Lucky for him, his Uncle Bill had been willing to step in and run Bigsby's Five & Dime. Caleb inherited the store from his father, who had inherited it from his father...Bigsby Duncan. Bill had been a lifesaver, his commitment to the store allowing Caleb the ability to stay home with Joelle.

"Well, maybe we can make something special for dinner tonight. Like grilled cheese sandwiches and tomato soup...your favorites," Caleb said, glancing down at his daughter only to discover she was no longer walking beside him.

Caleb froze, his heart pounding in his chest as he searched the area. Joelle had been walking beside him a minute ago and couldn't have gone far. Terror struck him as he remembered the dangerous attraction of the pond. It wasn't deep, but there was plenty enough for a child to drown. And then there was the flock of Canada geese that would bite if she got too close.

Seconds later, he spotted Joelle running toward the pond. "Joelle, stop," he hollered, moving as fast as he could to catch up with his daughter.

Although keeping his attention on Joelle, he couldn't help but notice the blonde-haired woman throwing a ball to play fetch with her dog. To his relief, Joelle stopped running a safe distance from the pond. She picked up the dog's ball and ran toward the water.

"Stop, Joelle," he shouted, closing the distance between them. No good ever came from dwelling on the past, and this time it had given his head-strong daughter the chance to chase after her own kind of fun.

Joelle tossed the ball into the pond and the dog lunged forward after it, then swam a few feet from shore to retrieve the ball.

"You know better than to run off like that," he said, taking his daughter by the hand and leading her away from the water's edge.

"I wanted to throw the ball for the doggy like the lady did. Did you see how good I threw it, Daddy?"

Sometimes it was like a lost cause trying to explain things, and this felt like one of them. He kneeled next to Joelle and gave her a hug, satisfied she was safe. "You threw it good, sweetheart. Maybe we should add that to our list of fun things to do."

"Yay. I like to play ball. And chase. And hide-go-seek. Can we do those things at home, Daddy?"

"I don't see why not." He picked Joelle up, settling her on his hip. He turned to apologize to the pretty woman as the big red dog bounded in their direction.

***

The little girl had come out of nowhere, surprising Madison. Especially given she didn't immediately see anyone racing after the child. Luckily, Freida was a bigger attraction than the pond. Madison hadn't been able to stop the child from throwing the ball, but it would seem there was nothing to fret about.

Well, all except..."Watch out," she called, trying to warn the man and his daughter as Frieda stopped next to them and dropped to roll on the ground. "She's going to shake. Frieda, no!" The Irish Setter's long hair would give a good dousing to anyone within distance if they didn't give the dog a wide berth. A fact Madison knew from an earlier experience this week with Frieda while taking her out for one of their twice daily dog-walking sessions.

Startled, the man spun around and looked at her just in time to see the dog go into action, but not enough time to spin back around. Unfortunately, that also meant the pair of them got all muddy because of all the rain they'd had the past couple of days.

"Freida, come." Madison moved to hook the leash on the dog's collar. "I'm so sorry..." The rest of the words failed her as she recognized the man. Not just any man. Her childhood crush. Her friend's husband. Correction...her friend's widowed husband. Madison swallowed hard, willing the words to come forth.

"Any dog with that much fur should come with a warning sign," he said, wiping a hand across his face and then trying to brush some of the mud from his daughter's face. But instead of making things better, he only smeared the mud splotches. The dry tone of his voice sounded as though he were serious. It was just a little muddy water, for heaven's sake. And the Caleb Duncan she remembered would have found humor in the situation.

"Probably. I'm so sorry." She searched in her handbag for something to help him clean away the dirt. "Here." Madison held out a couple of napkins she had stuffed there after her fast-food lunch. One never knew when extras would come in handy, and today, she was thankful for the old habit.

"Thanks." He wiped his daughter's face and then his own, but the napkins fell apart into little useless wet balls.

The little girl laughed. "You look funny, Daddy."

Caleb grimaced. "I'm glad you think so. You're not looking much better to tell you the truth." He turned back to Madison, his brow lines deepening as though perplexed. "Don't I know you?"

Madison shifted uncomfortably. "Sort of." Considering she was the one who had introduced him to Lauren. True, the guy was only an acquaintance, but it hadn't kept Madison from secretly having a crush on the slightly older, but oh, so handsome, son of Mr. Duncan. Caleb was at least five years older than they were, but to a high school senior he was Mr. Dreamy. Except, from the minute that she had introduced Lauren to Caleb, those two had eyes for no one else. Her friend never even knew Madison had a crush on Caleb, and of course, once those two were an item, the school-girl crush was put on secret lock-down...forever.

Instead, Madison faded out of sight, eventually moving to the city in search of a career filled with the promise of more excitement than a small town could ever offer. "I knew Lauren," she said, figuring that was more than enough of a connection. "I'm so sorry about the mess," Madison said, reaching out to use the cuff of her sleeve to wipe away a spot on his forehead that he missed.

Caleb frowned but hadn't moved. It was the distant look in his expression that did her in. He hadn't been able to place her identity, more than enough proof he had barely known of her existence. It had always been Lauren, and by the looks of things, still was, considering the wedding ring he wore a year and a half later.

"Madison Bradley. We met at your dad's store once and then you came home from college and volunteered to chaperone the senior high school prom. I introduced you to Lauren there."

"Oh, I remember you," Caleb said, his voice laced with pain as though the mere mention of Lauren's name had the power to hurt him.

"You knew my mommy?" Joelle asked, her blue eyes like wide saucers as she gazed up at Madison.

"I did. She was one of my friends in high school, and always the sunlight in a room." Lauren had been one of those glass is half full people...a positive can-do attitude toward everything.

"I miss her." Joelle pouted, tears welling in her eyes.

"I'm sure you do, honey. But your mommy is always in your heart, so look there next time you want to talk to her." It was the same thing her mother had told Madison when her father had died. She turned to Caleb. "Listen, let me offer you some free dog-walking or pet-transportation services. It's the least I can do to apologize."

Caleb shook his head. "There's only one problem. We don't have a dog... or a pet. Besides, your apology is accepted." His warm smile went straight to her heart, thrusting her back in time to make her feel like a giddy teenager again.

"I want a doggy, but Daddy keeps telling me no. You have a really big dog and I like him a lot because he loves to play."

"Freida is rather large, but she isn't my dog. I've just moved back to town from New York City, and I started offering pet sitting, dog walking, and animal transportation services. I'm trying to drum up some business," Madison said, handing him a card. "Since you don't have a dog, send me your dry-cleaning bill. I really am sorry about the mess."

"Honestly, it's not your fault. Joelle threw the ball into the water. We were just leaving before the rainstorm hits," he said, glancing up at the sky.

"The rain could wash all the mud off," Madison teased, trying to see the humor in the situation.

"It could, but I'd be more worried about a lightning storm popping up. We need to get to safety before that happens." Caleb took Joelle by the hand, prepared to make a run for it if necessary.

"But they aren't calling for thunder and lightning last I checked."

"The meteorologists don't always get it right. Better safe than sorry. It was nice running into you again." Caleb was down to earth and practical.

Starchy almost. And nothing like the adventure seeking pair he and Lauren had once been. It was as though Lauren's death had sucked the life from him.

"You too." *Awkward, but nice.* Madison's guilt at not having returned for her friend's funeral was equally troubling and had surfaced when she recognized Caleb. She should never have put her fashion career first, especially given that Julia, the owner of J'Taime Fashions had promised her the moon, only to under-deliver. And it had been Julia who threatened firing her if she left to come home after Lauren died.

Madison had been nothing more than a glorified gopher assistant who ran errands and reconciled the financial statements since Julia was a highly private woman and trusted her. But in five years, her boss never reviewed her designs with more than a cursory scan, dismissing them out of hand. It was also the reason Madison finally had the gumption to up and quit. Having returned to Dover to regroup, she was living with her mother and hoping to find a new job to use her design skills more effectively.

"Bye, Madison," Joelle said, waving.

"Bye, sweetie." The little girl was cute as a button and the spitting image of her mother with her sandy blonde hair and big blue eyes. Lauren would have loved her daughter to the moon and back, and it was a shame she wouldn't be here to watch her grow up. At least Caleb seemed quite loving...although more than a little over-protective.

Chapter Two

T alk about awkward with a capital A. Running into Madison after all these years had taken Caleb by surprise when he first drew close enough to see and vaguely recognize her. When she introduced herself, the memories all came back.

Caleb hadn't even known Madison left town, but then once he met Lauren, his whole life centered on her. The fact she didn't live in Dover, or even in the area, explained why he hadn't seen her at Lauren's funeral. And the big, hairy dog...that could be none other than the Granger's four-legged prize canine and it made sense they'd hired someone to help with the rambunctious Irish Setter.

Freida would be a handful for anyone, although Joelle didn't seem to mind as she played with the dog. The smiles on her face had been genuine and were accompanied by deep-down honest to goodness laughter...something Caleb hadn't seen much of since Lauren died. It's not that he didn't try to make his daughter happy. In fact, his priorities were her safety and happiness.

The clouds opened and poured out the rain, the sound like that of a jackhammer against the roof of the truck. Caleb pulled into the driveway, up close to the house. "Joelle, let's wait a few minutes to see if this lets up a bit."

"Okay, Daddy. That's a lot of rain."

"Want to play the I-Spy game while we wait? You can climb in the front seat with me," he said, glad they hadn't been caught out in the nasty weather. Muddy was easy enough to fix with a shower. Soaked to the bone, not so much, especially if one of them turned up sick.

Joelle unbuckled herself from the booster, came barreling over the center console, and scooted into the front passenger seat. "*Nah*. We always play that. Can I go out and play in the rain? I see kids do it on TV and it looks like so much fun."

"Sorry, honey. It could start storming with thunder and lightning, and that would be dangerous. Not only that, but one of us might get a nasty cold and that would be miserable." His daughter's sullen expression was a 180-degree turn from earlier, but it couldn't be helped. One day she would understand the word "no" kept her safe...because he loved her.

Except loving Lauren hadn't saved his wife from the dangers in life.

Maybe if they had taken a different route. Or if he had cleared the fallen tree from the path sooner. Then the snake wouldn't have been curled up, sunning itself in a crook. And it wouldn't have startled her horse, causing her to come unseated with a tragic ending.

"The rain is letting up," Joelle pointed out, bringing Caleb's attention back to the moment.

"A little, but perhaps we should make a run for it while we can. Follow me." Caleb slid out of the truck and held the door open, assisting Joelle out of the vehicle. Picking her up into his arms, he ran to the front porch and out of the rain, getting soaked in the short time to get there. Next time, he'd remember to grab an umbrella. It would certainly be his fault if Joelle caught a cold. He unlocked the front door, eager to get them inside and into some dry clothes.

Caleb flipped on the light switch, but nothing happened. He toggled the switch a few more times, but to no avail. "It looks like the power is out from the storm. It must have brought a tree down somewhere on a main power box. I need to call it in to the electric company but let me check the breaker box on our house and some of the other lights, to be sure." He set his daughter down, hoping the outage wouldn't last long.

"Can I watch TV while you check?" Joelle asked, uninterested in grown-up talk.

"Sorry. The television runs on electricity...so no electricity...no TV. Why don't you head to your room and grab some dry pants and a shirt? I can help you get dressed if you need me to." One of these days, he needed to have a generator installed, something else to add to the ever-growing to-do list.

Joelle scrunched up her face and shook her head. "I'm a big girl and can get dressed on my own. It's only when there's really hard zippers or buttons," she declared, moving toward the hall and disappearing.

Caleb headed to the utility room. The breakers all checked out fine, and it was all the lights in the house that were out. He searched his contacts and clicked on the power company entry.

"Generation Electric. How can I help you?" the crisp voice of an older woman asked.

"Good afternoon. I'd like to report a total power outage at 2651 Peabody Lane," Caleb said, glancing out at the now drizzling rain.

"Hold one second while I check this out. You're the only one to call this in so far, Mr. Duncan. Let me start a report and I'll have someone check into this for you. It shouldn't take long for us to dispatch someone to your location."

"Thank you," Caleb said, moving down the hall to check on Joelle, and stopping at her bedroom door. "The electric company is sending someone out to fix our power and it shouldn't be long. Do you want to build a tent in your room while we wait?" His daughter loved it when they built a tent, and he hung stars from the ceiling. She found comfort having the night sky close as she said her prayers, knowing her mother was in heaven. "Okay. Let's use the blue sheets. They're so pretty." They were also the color of his daughter's eyes. And Lauren's.

"Deal." Caleb pulled the stack of flat sheets from the hall closet and laid them on her bed. One by one, he stretched them out, tying twine on the corners to secure them at strategic points. Joelle draped one sheet around her back and ran around the room playing Queen of the Forest.

His phone rang, and it was the power company. It hadn't taken long for them to call back. "Hello. Did you find the problem?" Caleb asked.

"We did. Unfortunately, it's not a problem for our repair team," the woman said, her answer more than a little vague.

"What do you mean?"

"The problem is an unpaid electric bill. It would seem, Mr. Duncan, that your account is over sixty-days past due."

Caleb frowned, glancing down at the phone as if he could see the woman on the other end and would get better answers. "Overdue? That's not possible. I've got it set up on auto draft every month to pay the balance."

"I'm sorry, but there's nothing I can do on my end. Give the main office a call and see if you can get this sorted out," the woman said, absolving herself from any ability to help.

"I'll do that. This is utterly ridiculous," he snapped. Ever since Lauren died and life seemed to drift out of control, he had put measures into place to keep things like this from happening. True, he didn't bother with his mail, instead piling it up in a box that he took care of when he was good and ready, but it didn't mean things didn't get done. There was never anything of importance, anyway, mostly junk mail.

In a small town, if someone wanted him for something...they simply called or stopped by to ask. Caleb dialed the main office, the automated system placing him on hold.

"What's wrong, Daddy?" Joelle asked.

"Nothing, sweetheart. Just a little mix-up. I'll have it sorted out in a jiffy." He hoped anyway. They had to be wrong. Caleb made his way down the hall, stopping at his desk in the corner of the spare bedroom. He skimmed through the stack of mail, stopping on the one from the electric company. Slicing the envelope open, he unfolded the letter.

Overdue. The big red stamp on the top caught his attention immediately. Still, there had to be some mistake. It would seem it wasn't the power company's fault at all. Which left the bank, as clearly his auto draft stopped sending in the payments. Hopefully, it was only the power bill, otherwise he was about to have a gigantic mess on his hands.

Caleb hung up the phone, no longer needing to talk to the rep. He called the bank instead, intent on understanding the problem.

"Sunrise Select Bank. How may I help you?" the woman asked.

"This is Caleb Duncan and there seems to be a problem with my account. I've got an auto draft set up for my electric bills and yet they seem to have stopped paying and my power was cut off."

"I'm sorry Mr. Duncan. Let me check into this for you." After verifying his information, the woman made a few comments along the way, letting him know she was still investigating the issue. "I found the problem. There's not enough money in your account to cover the payment. You have a negative balance with some charges and late fees."

"That's impossible," Caleb fumed. "My uncle makes the store deposits like clockwork and there shouldn't be a problem." He massaged his temples, hoping to stop the pounding that throbbed in his ears as the woman's words sunk in.

"Yes, the deposits come in every week. But they aren't enough to cover your expenses anymore. It would seem they are getting less and less each time. We need you to come to the bank as soon as possible to clear this up and deposit some additional funds. Is there anything else I can do to help you, Mr. Duncan?" she asked.

This was ludicrous. "No." Talking to the woman wouldn't change a thing, and he hung up the phone. Apparently, only money could fix his current situation. Caleb didn't have a clue what was going on at the store or why the deposits were shrinking. For sixteen months, his uncle had handled the store business, but if the deposits were less, it could only mean one thing...the store was in financial trouble.

After making sure Joelle was fine, he called the store, relieved when his uncle answered the phone.

"Hey, it's Caleb."

"Good afternoon. Is something wrong? You don't normally call in, so I'm a little surprised to hear from you." They weren't close, but they were family. And if it hadn't been for his uncle, Caleb might not have been able to keep the family business going after Lauren died.

"There's seems to be a problem at the bank. To make a long story short, my power got turned off because there's not enough money to pay the bills. What's going on at the store? The lady at the bank said the deposits are way down and not enough to cover my expenses." Caleb stopped pacing long enough to gaze out at the empty pasture. Miles and miles of fields and property that once brought him solace, but now mocked him because of the expense it cost him to keep the place.

"I was hoping things wouldn't come to this point, but I just don't know what else to do," Uncle Bill said. The comment threw Caleb for a loop because it almost sounded like his uncle knew there was an issue…and hadn't said a word to him.

"You know there's a problem? I'm still the owner of the store and have a right to know what's happening," Caleb said, unhappy with the turn of events.

"Business is off. Way off. And I've not said anything because I keep hoping to get the store back on track. I'm trying, just not with much success. Yet. I'm curious though, how is it you weren't aware? Don't you even balance your checkbook anymore?" he asked, shifting the topic to Caleb's shortcomings.

"No, not really. I just set everything up to autopay. You make the deposits; the auto drafts pay the bills. End of story." In hindsight, it wasn't the smartest plan. Or it would have been if he'd at least kept tabs on the situation. Early on, just getting up and through the day had taken all his energy and willpower, his focus on Joelle.

"It's past time you started joining the real world again. You can't hole up at the house with Joelle forever. What happens when she goes to school?" Uncle Bill asked.

All valid points. "You're right. And it doesn't look like I have that luxury anymore, does it?"

"I assume you have money from Lauren's insurance policy. Maybe you can use that to tide you over? And maybe it's time to consider selling the store."

"No. The insurance money is for Joelle's education. I've got some emergency money I can deposit in the bank, but it won't last long. And selling the store is out of the question. It's been in the family for generations, and I won't let my father down." He'd been groomed to take over the place, but it happened far sooner than planned. His parents' deaths were unexpected and heartbreaking. And then Lauren joined them in heaven, leaving him alone to raise Joelle and pray he made all the right decisions. It was a tough job and every day he faced the fear he would make a mistake. *Like the one with Lauren.*

"You might not have a choice, I'm sorry to say. Unless you can drum up more business. Competition is stiff and costs are rising."

Caleb ran a hand through his hair. His uncle's advice made sense...but how could he focus on the store and take care of Joelle at the same time? "Okay, thanks."

His uncle never married and never had children and wasn't a likely source for advice, but Pastor Kyle was another story entirely. Caleb called the church and was relieved to hear the Pastor was available. He trusted the man as a leader of the community, and a leader for the health and well-being of the people's spirituality and faith.

"Pastor Kyle Lawrence," the older man answered the phone.

"Good afternoon. This is Caleb Duncan. I've got a problem and I hope you can help me."

"Of course. What's going on? Is Joelle okay?" the pastor asked.

"She's fine." Caleb relayed the story with as little information as possible but filling in the blanks enough for Pastor Kyle to know the significance of his ask. "I'm hoping you can recommend someone to watch Joelle while I spend some time at the store and try to figure things out."

"Son, you're in luck. I've got the perfect woman for the job. Her name is Madison Bradley. She just arrived back in town, and I know she's looking for work. Seems to me you two knew each other years ago. Let me get you her contact info," he offered.

Madison. No way. Of course, he remembered her considering he'd only just run into the woman at the park today. Madison came loaded with memories of Lauren, and Caleb wasn't sure he could handle the effect her presence would have on him.

Pastor Kyle came back on the line. "I've got her number. Do you have a pen to write it down?"

"Actually, do you have anyone else you could recommend? I mean, it's just that Madison and Lauren were friends, and it would be awkward." At least he could be honest with Pastor Kyle and share his deepest thoughts, knowing the man wouldn't be sharing the information with anyone in town.

"Caleb, it's high time you move past your grief. Lauren wouldn't want you stuck in the past like this...afraid to live. Madison's perfect for Joelle, and for what you need."

As an employer...that's what the Pastor meant, right? If he didn't get the business in order, he'd lose it and the security of a home for Joelle, not to mention the home he'd shared with Lauren.

Resigned to the inevitable, Caleb let out a sigh. "I've already got her number because I ran into her today at the park. Thanks for your help." He rang off, unwilling to discuss the Pastor's comment in depth.

For months, people in town had tried to get him to come out from under the rock they claimed he was living under. *Find someone new, they said. You're still young.*

But they didn't understand.

A love like the one he shared with Lauren happened once in a lifetime. For him, there could never be another.

Chapter Three

♥

Madison moved the macaroni and cheese casserole into the oven and set the timer for thirty minutes. She had been craving the cheesy pasta concoction for months but had been unwilling to settle for the blue box at the store, even though it had been a childhood favorite. No, she wanted the real thing, and being at home with her mother provided her the time to prepare the dish. They both loved to cook, and it had always been fun to see what recipes they would decide to make...the harder, the better. The meals didn't always turn out, some rather inedible, but the memories of the time spent with her mother would last a lifetime. It was times like these Madison had missed the most when she moved to New York City.

Her mother had been disappointed and worried when she left, but she also understood there wasn't much call for a fashion designer in Dover. The opportunity to work in one of the fashion capitals of the world had been exciting and not an offer she would ever turn down. But back in town, at least for the time being, Madison was finding a much-needed respite from the fast-paced life.

"So, what's on your agenda for the rest of tonight?" her mother asked as she tidied the kitchen.

"Just dinner with you and then I plan to curl up on the recliner with my favorite plush pink blanket and a sweet romance story to warm my heart. You know me and my happily ever-after books." Madison laughed.

"I do at that. I remember when you used to sit on the old wooden bench outside the library and read all day," her mother said, her eyes lit with a teasing glow.

"Did you know that one day I read six Barbara Cartland books?"

"I seemed to remember you telling me that, now that you mention it. Reading kept you out of trouble, so I didn't mind. I was surprised you didn't become a writer. You've always been so creative, no matter what you put your mind to doing."

"Thanks, Mom. I was tempted to try once, but I kept doodling dress designs while I tried to figure out what to write." It was then Madison knew her true calling.

Her mother nodded. "I think you would be good at anything you set your heart on doing."

Except she wasn't doing anything of the sort now. "Thanks for the vote of confidence, Mom. If I would have known how hard it would be to break into the business—"

"You would have still gone after your dreams. You take after your father. Anything that man set his mind to doing, he was all in."

"True. I remember when I wanted a fort in the backyard, and he went out straight away and bought a two-room kit. We spent a solid week building it together. Mostly him, but it was fun. Coolest fort ever." Her father had been loving and supportive, and always put her mother and her at the top of his priority list.

"You should go up there and read tonight...it was always your favorite place."

"Not a bad idea. Thanks. Hope I can still climb the ladder…and that I fit," Madison said with a chuckle. All her favorite posters hung on the walls, as well as many of her earlier dress designs. Her place of peace once upon a time.

"I'm sure you'll be just—" The doorbell rang, cutting her mother off mid-sentence as they looked toward the living room. It's not like they were expecting anyone. Her mother rinsed her hands.

"I'll see who it is. Probably just a door-to-door salesperson we need to send promptly on their way," Madison said, more than ready to handle whoever landed on their doorstep. Whatever it was, they weren't buying.

She pulled open the front door and swore her eyes were playing tricks on her. "Caleb?" It came out as a question even though she knew for a fact it was him. "Come in," she offered, once she recovered from the shock.

"Sorry, I can't." Caleb's gaze darted to his truck. "Joelle is with me, and I've only got a minute."

"I see," Madison said, her gaze drifting toward the black truck parked in the driveway.

Joelle waved, and Madison waved back at the sweet little girl. It was more than a little heart-breaking to think Joelle would grow up without her mother. Lauren always thought of life as an adventure, and kids and family were all part of it.

Madison returned her focus to Caleb, curious why he was here. "How can I help you? Have you reconsidered and come to give me a dry-cleaning bill?" she teased.

"No, I think a washing machine will do the trick. But if you insist on making amends, perhaps you'll say yes to my proposition." She had the distinct impression he wasn't overly excited about being here, which only confused her more.

Caleb, her childhood crush, wanted something...from her. *Yes.* Her heart answered as it raced at high speed. For one split second, the idea of doing something with him or for him catapulted her back to high school. A time when she dreamed of him asking her out. At eighteen, having a secret crush was the 'in' thing for girls. "I've never been propositioned." Madison smiled, using humor to ground her wayward emotions.

"There's always a first. The thing is...something has come up at the store and I need a sitter for

Joelle. Well, it's more like a nanny. Full-time. Every day." Caleb ran a hand through his hair, more proof he wasn't comfortable with the request.

"I don't understand. Who will take care of her now? Did they quit? I mean, this seems kind of sudden." Nervous energy bubbled and rose to the top and left Madison babbling.

Caleb frowned. "There is no one else. I've been taking care of Joelle since her mother passed away. It's just the two of us and I'm very protective of my daughter and who's around her. Like I said, there's a problem at the store that I need to handle, and I can't very well take care of Joelle and be at the store all the time."

This was a side of Caleb she'd glimpsed at the park, but it would seem he was living a life beyond over-protective. "Why me?" she asked.

Caleb shoved his hands in his front jeans pocket, his gaze landing on the truck once again as though to reassure himself Joelle was okay. "Pastor Kyle recommended you. Not to mention, you and Lauren were friends, and Lauren was always a good judge of character."

Madison shrugged, knowing she could not change the outcome. "Thank you for thinking of me, but there's no way I can accept."

"I see," Caleb said, stepping off the porch. He stopped and turned back. "Why not? Please say yes, I've got to focus on saving the store. It's Joelle's family legacy, and our livelihood. I don't know who else I can turn to on such short notice." The desperation in his voice was almost enough for her to give in, but the past wouldn't go away, and she wasn't willing to test her resolve and tumble head long into crushing on Caleb again.

That night at the prom, Madison had foolishly thought she would tell Caleb how she felt about him, even though they'd only met once at the hardware store. In her dreams, they were a couple who lived happily ever after. But the reality was he had fallen in love with Lauren.

"I can't. Perhaps Mrs. Forester's daughter can watch Joelle. She's in the tenth grade and off for the summer," Madison suggested.

"No. I don't know her, and I don't trust that she could do the job as well as I would expect. I can't take any chances. Thanks anyway." Caleb turned and headed to his truck. Without so much as a glance, he backed out of the driveway and left.

Madison hated to tell him no, especially given Bigsby's was in trouble. But the whole situation screamed awkward, and there simply wasn't any way to safeguard her heart a second time around. The older Caleb was more handsome than ever, even if he was more reserved. But then, life had dealt him some lemons and perhaps everything was still sour. Caleb was still grieving for his wife.

As for Madison, she feared that having once spent months to get over her childhood crush, it would be ten times worse getting over an adult crush. If it were even possible. She had a feeling if she let her emotions run wild, it wouldn't take much to start imagining a life with Caleb Duncan all over again.

Something she absolutely would not do.

Chapter Four

♥

Caleb took his daughter by the hand and walked the short distance from the parking spot to the store. With no one to watch Joelle, there was no other choice but to bring her with him. Trying to figure out the problem and fix it would be next to impossible with an active child around. The dolls and toys he brought should keep her occupied for a while.

"Let's go behind the counter and find you a nice, cozy spot to play. A tea party with your dolls sounds like fun, or maybe they can be doctors and nurses today." Caleb opened a blanket and spread it out, dropping the backpack in the middle.

"Okay, Daddy. We never come to the store, so this will be loads of fun."

"Except you need to stay right here and be a good girl while I look around and talk to Uncle Bill."

Joelle's attention had already shifted to her dolls, but hopefully, his message registered. A movement off to the side of the store caught Caleb's attention and he spotted Tommy, the only other employee at Bigsby's.

"Good morning, Mr. Duncan. What brings you in today? Is there something I can round up for you?" he asked as he headed for the register. The kid was in his early twenties, had clean-cut hair, and his family had been in town for ages. Caleb had hired the boy right out of high school, and he'd been working there for over five years.

"Good morning, Tommy. Thanks for the offer, but I'm not shopping. Business is down and I wanted to have a look around and see what I can do to make some changes." The details weren't anything Caleb wanted to disclose, preferring to keep his private affairs out of the gossip chain.

"That stinks, but honestly, I hadn't noticed. Is there anything I can do to help?" The kid shuffled some papers on the counter, looking anywhere but at Caleb.

"No, not right now, anyway. I'll keep you posted if anything changes." Maybe Caleb was desperate for answers, but Tommy's sudden change in demeanor hadn't gone unnoticed. To the best of his knowledge, Tommy was a good kid from a wonderful family. He didn't like to think the boy would do anything illegal or hurt the store. But this early in his assessment, Caleb wouldn't rule anything out, including an employee helping themselves to the nightly till. It would explain the low deposits but be a seriously bold move. And one that would be easily traceable, which is why the ledgers were the best place for Caleb to start.

At least those files were something he could take home to work on, though it would still be difficult with Joelle requiring most of his attention. Focus would be key and not a luxury he would be afforded until after his daughter had gone to bed in the evenings.

His uncle came out of the back office and headed their way. Dressed in jeans and a polo shirt, his mother's brother walked with an air of confidence. He was meticulous about his appearance, right down to the weekly trimmings of his short gray hair. Even as the weathered lines on his face grew more prominent, they only made his uncle more distinguished. "Good morning, Joelle. How's my little angel?" he asked, kneeling next to her.

Joelle jumped to her feet and ran to hug her uncle. "I'm not an angel," she said, giggling.

"To me you are," Uncle Bill said, shooting her a wink.

"Angels are pretty." Joelle's eyes were wide with wonder.

"Exactly." His uncle nipped her nose, laughing as Joelle ran back to play. "I'm guessing you're here because of what we talked about yesterday?" Uncle Bill shot a cursory glance at Tommy.

"I am. Everything should be back to normal at the house within a couple of hours, but I need to get to the root of the problem." Caleb had stopped at the bank before coming here and made a rather large deposit, authorizing all back payments to be made current. Then a call to the electric company reassured him they would turn his power back on.

"Tommy, why don't you start stocking the shelves with the new inventory delivered yesterday?" his uncle said.

"Yes, sir," Tommy said, shuffling off to do his work, but not before shooting Caleb a strange look. Whether it was a message or fear, Caleb couldn't tell, but he'd be sure to talk to the kid later.

"I figured you'd rather not air your financial problems in front of the help. Besides, something has been going on with him lately and he's been acting different. Tense. Jumpy almost." Deep grooves lined his uncle's forehead, his finger tapping on the counter rapidly as though trying to figure out the source of unease.

Caleb was inclined to agree with his uncle's assessment of the kid. "I also thought he was acting unusual, but I'm sure it's nothing to do with the store. Tommy's been working here a long time and I remember him as an outstanding employee. But to be on the safe side, we should keep a closer eye on him. At least for the near future."

His uncle nodded. "Will do."

"And thanks for keeping quiet about the financial issues I'm having. It's one thing for people to know business is down, quite another for them to find out I started bouncing payments all over town. It won't be long, and everyone will know anyway, what with the active gossipmongers in Dover. The longer I can stave off the inevitable, the better. Maybe by then, it will all be fixed."

"I feel awful that this happened on my watch. I'm sorry. I'm fresh out of ideas on how to drum up business, but open to any suggestions you might offer. Though maybe it's the new drugstore in Norwich that's stealing our customers." His uncle was upset with the way things were going, but in the end, it wasn't his fault. The responsibility for keeping the store profitable was in Caleb's hands.

"No need to apologize. I should have been paying closer attention. I owe you big time for stepping in and taking care of things for me after Lauren died. I just wasn't up to being a parent and running the store...not without Lauren by my side. Unfortunately, if you're right about the store in Norwich, then I'm in big trouble. If this keeps up, not only will I lose the store, but I'll lose our house as the two properties were tied together in a refinance loan years ago when Dad was alive." He'd been meaning to separate the loans for years, knowing it wasn't a suitable business model. But his life got super busy with a wife and child, and it was one of those things that simply never happened. And based on what was happening now, there wasn't a bank out there that would take the risk.

"If anyone can fix what's wrong, I'm sure you'll figure it out."

"Thanks. Can you print out the last eighteen months' worth of inventory and expense ledgers? It's as good as any place to look for places to cut back." The store's record-keeping was antiquated, but at least Caleb had gotten everything into a computer system a couple of years ago. It wasn't ideal but would do in a pinch. It sure beat trying to decipher handwritten ledgers.

Uncle Bill nodded. "I'll get right on it, but it might take me a day or two. That's a lot of records."

The overhead bell on the front door jingled, signaling a customer had arrived. "Thanks. We can talk more later," Caleb said. His uncle headed for the office, leaving him to deal with the customer since Tommy was still in the backroom. Not a good policy and one to make note of that needed changing, as someone should always be on hand to greet the customers.

Caleb turned to face the newcomer but didn't see anyone. He scanned the entire store, but there wasn't a soul in the place, which made no sense. Leaning over the counter, he checked on Joelle, only to discover she wasn't sitting on her blanket, or anywhere in sight. Adrenaline coursed through his body, his heart pounding. He bolted for the front door, fear driving his every step.

The bell didn't ring by itself.

Madison made her way through town on the way to a client's house to pick up a dog. It was a new client, and she'd been hired for the hour to take the dog to the park. The light turned red at the Main Street intersection, and she came to a stop. Of course, there was no one else at the light. A light that almost seemed silly given the size of the town. She tapped her fingers on the steering wheel, beating out the rhythm of the country song on the radio.

Minutes passed, but still, the light didn't change. She edged forward, wondering if it was one of the motion trip sensors to signal the need for a light change. Still nothing. If the light wasn't working, she'd be here all day and miss her client appointment.

Taking her foot off the brake, she inched forward, checking in all directions. No traffic. No issue. Madison pressed the accelerator. Her car chugged in response, and then the motor shut off, the red engine warning light flashing on the dashboard.

What the heck was going on? This was the worst possible moment for car trouble. Actually, there was no good time for car trouble. Nellie had been with Madison since high school, and she loved the car dearly. The Buick was old but had been a suitable vehicle over the years. At some point, she needed to get a new pre-owned car, but right now, there was barely money to pay her bills, much less a car loan. It was on her someday soon list.

Which did her no good now. She tried to restart the car, to no avail. *Why me, Lord?* Broken down and blocking the intersection, and soon to be late for her appointment. Talk about having a bad day.

Madison turned on the flashers to alert any other vehicle approaching that she was having trouble. She got out of the car and raised the hood before moving to the sidewalk, following all the safety rules drummed into her by her father. He died ten years ago, and she missed him dearly. Especially during times like this. What she wouldn't give to be able to call him for help.

A car was not something she could afford and asking her mother for a loan was out of the question. Madison was too old not to handle her affairs, especially given she quit her job before she had another one. Another life lesson she had been taught, but not the one she had followed. For her, it had been the dream she chased, not reality.

Madison let out a deep breath and tried to regroup. She called the local garage and spoke with the mechanic who had nothing but more bad news. His best guess was her worst nightmare. Several possibilities and most would set her back more than she could afford. Bye-bye doggy clientele. The mechanic assured her he would send a tow truck but couldn't promise her when they would arrive, as there was another tow scheduled ahead of hers.

She called her client to apprise her of the change in plans, and of course, the woman fired her on the spot. The dog needed a walk, and she would find someone who could handle the job. It would be the same with all her new clients. All three of them, that is.

Madison closed her eyes and rubbed her forehead. "Nothing like being flat broke to make one see things clearly," she said out loud, more than a little frustrated.

A tug on the pant leg of her jeans startled her, and she was surprised to see Joelle. She kneeled next to the little girl, who was smiling at her. "Hi, Joelle. I didn't expect to see you here." Madison looked all around, but there was no sign of Caleb.

"Hi, Miss Madison. I looked through the window and saw you talking on the phone," Joelle said, her voice soft and sweet.

"Where's your dad?"

"Working on stuff in the store," the little girl said, pointing at Bigsby's.

Madison peered at the store and then back at Joelle. There was no way Caleb would have let his daughter come out here on her own. "Why don't you and I go see your dad? I'm sure he's wondering where you went." She would only be a couple of minutes, so hopefully, the tow truck didn't show up and leave. Of course, the way her day had started, nothing would surprise her at this point.

"Okey dokey," Joelle said, taking Madison's hand and happily skipping her way back to the store.

They hadn't gone but two steps when Caleb came running toward them. He drew up short when he spotted Madison, but his gaze dropped to his daughter. Pulling her up into his arms, he hugged her tight. "Thank goodness you're all right. You gave me quite a scare, young lady."

"Sorry, Daddy. I saw Miss Madison, and she's broken down. I think she was crying."

Madison had no idea what the crying thing was about, but the broken part was spot on.

Caleb's gaze shifted to Madison. "*Umm*, how are you broken? Did you fall or something? Is that why you were crying?" he asked. His concern was touching, even if a little off base.

"Or something. My car broke down. As to the crying, let's just say this would be a good time for tears, but I'm too upset for such nonsense at the moment. I have had this car forever and it's never given me any trouble. The mechanic mentioned it could be as simple as a bad battery. The other possibility could be a faulty alternator or fuel pump."

Caleb smiled. "I'm sorry you're having issues with your car. Is there anything I can do?"

"Thanks, but I've got a tow truck coming." What she would do after it came and towed her car, she wasn't sure, but she'd figure out the next step when she got to it. All she could handle right now was one thing at a time.

"She needs money, Daddy. I heard her say she's broke and busted," Joelle said.

Madison covered her mouth with one hand, surprise and dismay all wrapped into one as she realized Joelle had overheard her remark. And now, to her mortification...Caleb knew. Even if Joelle messed up the repeat, any adult would know exactly what it meant.

Caleb quirked an eyebrow up at her. "If it's money you need, I've got a job opening that's still yours for the taking." And just like that, they were back to yesterday's conversation.

It was on the tip of her tongue to say no, but at what point did she stop making her problems worse and latch on to a bit of good fortune when it came her way? It's not like Caleb was looking for a relationship or love, so maybe it would be easier to protect her heart than she thought. After all, the man had been her friend's husband.

Forget the rest. Her childhood crush was long over and everything that stood between them would keep it that way. "I'll take your job offer on one condition."

"What's that?" he asked, his expression one of genuine relief. But then he hadn't heard her condition yet.

"That you understand I'm leaving as soon as I find a job. This is short term, not a career move."

Caleb nodded. "I'll take the condition, but I've got one of my own."

"What's that?" she asked, mimicking him.

"You start now. I turned my back for a few minutes and Joelle wound up out on the street. This could have been disastrous. There's no way I can juggle the work I need to do at the store and watch her as carefully as I should." He ran a hand through his hair and then rubbed the back of his neck as though the tension had been too much.

"Lucky for everyone, nothing happened. And yes, right after the tow truck arrives, I'll take over with Joelle. It works, seeing as my new client just fired me. For some off-the-wall reason, they want their dog walker to *actually* walk the dog," she teased, finding another tidbit of humor in the situation.

Chapter Five

♥

"**G**uess what, sweetheart? Miss Madison is going to be your new nanny. So, you better be on your best behavior and no more of this running off whenever you want to. Daddy can't keep you safe when you wander away, and neither can Miss Madison."

Relying on someone else to protect and watch over Joelle didn't come easily to Caleb. So the more he impressed upon his daughter the need for good behavior, the better this might all work out. The bonus, however, was that he could work on balancing his bank statements from home. Which would then give him the chance to get comfortable leaving Joelle with the new nanny.

"Yay. You can play Barbie with me. And wait till you see my tent. Daddy made the best tent ever for me. He says it's blue like my eyes." Joelle giggled, pointing at her eyes to emphasize her point.

Madison grinned. "Sounds like a plan. I get paid to play."

"Well, I'm hoping as a nanny you'll do a little more than that around the house. Maybe I can talk you into cooking. It's not my strong suit, although, not from the lack of trying. I promise."

"Daddy and I cook stuff. But sometimes it's burnt, and we throw it away." Joelle's nose scrunched up in distaste.

"I'm sure we can arrange some actual work time in the day. So what's the plan?"

For the first time since he'd discovered his power was out, it appeared things were moving in a positive direction. Hopefully, his uncle was right, and he could save Bigsby's. "Let me run into the store for a minute and tell my uncle I'm leaving. He's working on printing out some ledger statements for me to review and should have them finished by tomorrow or the next day."

"Sounds good. It'll give me a chance to look around the store, seeing as I haven't been in since I came back to town while I keep an eye out for the tow truck. They should be here any minute, and I just need to give the driver the keys."

They headed inside, Joelle hand in hand with her new best and only nanny.

"Be right back." Caleb headed for the backroom, not seeing his uncle. Tommy was stocking shelves and waved in their direction, but otherwise kept to himself. He peeked into the office and found his uncle hard at work. "Hey there, I've got to run to the house. Turns out Madison Bradley needs a job and she's going to watch Joelle for me so I can focus more on the accounts and the store."

"Sounds like a plan. I'm sure once you've reviewed the ledgers, you'll figure something out that I'm doing wrong...or could do better. My failure isn't from the lack of trying to get it right," he added.

"Again, thank you for all you've done for Joelle and me. When you finish printing those out, can you drop them by the house? I'm thinking with a new nanny, I should work from home for the first few days just to see how it all pans out."

His uncle frowned, shaking his head. "What, you don't trust Madison? Or is this more about you not wanting to let Joelle out of your sight?

You know, at some point you are going to have to let loose of the tight control and let her live a little."

"Maybe, but not yet." Caleb turned, pausing at the doorway to watch Madison walk around the store, pointing out items to Joelle. The two of them laughed at something she said. Madison wore her emotions for all to see. Bubbly like a freshly popped bottle of champagne, the woman made the Easter Bunny seem slow. Straight blonde shoulder-length hair framed her pixie face. She was an attractive woman for sure, not that he was interested in any way other than as a professional.

Lauren was the light of his life and always would be. Some folks in town suggested it was time he moved on and started to live again, but he wasn't ready. Not that he would ever be ready because he still loved his wife as much now as the day he'd fallen hard for her. Death couldn't change the depth of feelings in his heart. Actually, it had strengthened them. Caleb's gaze dropped down to the ring on his left hand...the symbol of his love. The forever circle.

He pushed the thought aside and crossed the room to join them. "All set ladies?"

"Yup. Look at what Miss Madison found. *Umm*, what are they called again?" Joelle asked, her face scrunched up as she tried to remember.

"Pipe cleaners." Madison's smile was warm and bright, calming his first reaction to the identity of the fuzzy metal sticks.

"That's it." Joelle held up three packages, each in a different color.

"You're not planning on smoking around my daughter, are you?" Caleb teased, but in some small way, making sure.

Madison shook her head and laughed. "Hardly. They're for arts and crafts. Hence...the glue, sparkles, and fuzzy puff balls," she added, holding up the other items in her hand.

Which made far more sense given they were purple, green, and yellow. "Good." How was he supposed to know? It's not like he ever did much in the way of arts and crafts growing up, and certainly never anything that involved a pipe cleaner.

She headed for the checkout counter. "I gave the tow truck driver the keys while you were in the back office, so other than paying for this stuff, I'm all set to go."

"Tommy, put her items on my tab, please," Caleb said, unwilling to let her pay.

Madison turned back to him, wallet in hand. "You don't have to do that. I don't mind seeing as it's my idea."

"Neither do I, and since it's for Joelle, I insist." Not to mention, Madison had never refuted the broken and busted comment his daughter had relayed.

Moments later, Joelle carrying the bag of goodies, the three of them headed for the truck. On the way there, Caleb tried and barely got in a word or two, his daughter stealing the show. Her animated discussion revolved around what animal she would make with the pipe cleaners, and the list was endless.

Caleb turned into the long driveway and parked in front of the house. "Before you two run off and tackle your first crafting project, I'll show you around inside and outside to point out any areas of concern," Caleb offered. Places like the barn were off-limits. Outside without supervision. There was a long list he wanted to share with the new nanny.

"Sure thing. But just so you know…I know what a living room looks like, and a kitchen, and a bedroom, and maybe even a bathroom," she said, shooting him a wink. Madison's humor was cute and would keep him on his toes.

"Yes, but do you know where I keep the extra set of keys for the house? Or like, where dirty shoes go? Or even where to find an umbrella?" he asked, figuring two could play her game.

"Well, based on all that insanely important information, lead on." Madison chuckled.

Caleb unlocked the front door and gestured for them to enter. "Don't forget to show her my room, Daddy. It's a fairy princess room. And you got to show her the tent," Joelle said, beaming with pride as she grabbed Madison's hand to lead her down the hall.

Caleb nodded. "Maybe you can show her your room and the tent later. While I'm working." The tent and stars were something he and Lauren had started when Joelle was two years old. It was their special thing and not something he felt inclined to share with another woman. Lauren's friend or otherwise.

As they walked from room to room, Caleb covered what he thought was most important. Stopping at the back door of the kitchen, he reached up to grab a set of car keys and held them out to Madison. "While you're here, you can use the black car under the carport. At least until your vehicle is fixed."

Madison smiled. "Really? Wow! I won't say no to your generous offer. Thank you so much, and it will make things easier to get here and go home every day."

It hadn't been a simple decision to make, but it had been the right one. The black car had been Lauren's and other than driving it around the property to keep it running smoothly, it wasn't used. Also, it would be better if he wasn't playing chauffeur the whole time Madison was the nanny. They stepped out onto the porch. "It's that one right over there," he said, pointing toward the carport on the house side of the barn.

"Perfect. Thanks again."

Caleb barely heard her answer, his focus on the truck and horse trailer pulling out onto the road from his driveway. He hadn't been expecting anyone, and he certainly didn't use the barn for anything. Perhaps someone turning around, except if that were true, they were going in the wrong direction based on the way they were facing and would have come from.

"What's wrong?" Madison asked, following him off the porch.

"I'm going to check out the barn. I can't imagine who that was or what they were doing and why they didn't stick around to talk to me." The man had jumped into the truck and drove off the second he spotted them.

Madison and Joelle followed him, but a sense of urgency had Caleb in a near run. Something wasn't right. He pulled open the barn door, the fresh scent of hay assailing him. Which made no sense considering he hadn't used the barn since Lauren's riding accident, and he had sold the horses.

Once upon a time, he loved riding horses, but no more.

Not now. Not ever.

He rounded the corner into the first corridor and stopped short. Caleb shook his head and tried to clear his vision because none of what he saw made sense. A sleek, all-white mare that stood about fourteen hands high was tied to the post.

"Daddy, she's beautiful," Joelle said, running toward the horse.

"Joelle, no! Get back. It's not safe," he warned. Caleb didn't have a clue what was going on, but he intended to find out.

His daughter stopped in her tracks, her eyes wide with fear. She backed up and moved to stand next to Madison, grabbing her hand for comfort. "Where did the horse come from, Daddy?"

"I have no idea, but once we find out…it's going straight back. Someone dropped it off, probably hoping I'd take the horse in as a freeloader. They picked the wrong place, that's all I'm saying."

"If that was the case, why would they leave hay, feed, and tack?" Madison asked, picking Joelle up in her arms and moving closer.

The mare sniffed at his clothes and then nudged his shoulder as if trying to get Caleb's attention. She was elegant and well balanced, and certainly not someone's cast off.

"She likes you, Daddy." Joelle giggled.

"Look, Caleb...there's an envelope stapled to the post where the mare's tied," Madison said, pointing toward the stall.

Sure enough, Madison was right. Caleb moved forward, ignoring the horse and snatched the envelope off the post. He tore it open and pulled out the letter inside.

"What's it say? Read it out loud as you've got me more than a little curious," Madison asked.

Caleb skimmed over the page, some words popping out at him, but not making much sense. It sounded like someone had given him a horse. Which was ridiculous. *Or was it?*

"It says I've been chosen as the recipient of Sundancer's Star," he said, going back to the top of the page to read it out loud.

Sundancer's Legacy

Sundancer is a legendary mare who helped Arabella, an early American pioneer woman, find peace and love with her new Indian family hundreds of years ago. Legend has it, that the mare found Arabella after she had fallen sick and wandered off from her wagon train which left her be-

hind unknowingly. Finding Arabella near death, the mare led the warrior Tanveer to her. The brave warrior brought Arabella back to his teepee, and the women of the tribe nursed her back to health. Tanveer and Arabella fell in love, and he took her as his wife, giving her Sundancer as a wedding gift.

Over the years, Sundancer had many foals and Arabella gave them to other people based on two conditions. One, that all the descendant's first foals would bear the first name of Sundancer. And two, those foals could never be sold, only gifted to someone with a broken spirit who needed help.

The legacy still lives on in the hearts of those helped, but also in the horses who bring the gift of healing.

He finished reading and looked to Madison, trying to gauge her reaction before he continued. "There's a postscript at the end. It reads...*Sundancer's Star is yours for as long as you need her. She can't be sold, only gifted to someone in need if you choose not to keep her. The same would go for her first foal. May Sundancer's Legacy bring you peace in your heart, and happiness in your life. It's well known you once had a great love for horses. Now is your chance to rekindle the flame you once knew. Ride with the wind and be blessed."*

Caleb folded the letter back up and shoved it in his pocket. "I can't accept this gift, and I don't *want* this gift."

"I think it's an amazing story of love and triumph. Perhaps someone understands better than you do what you need to move forward in your life. I've not been around you much yet, but I can tell the past is holding you back." Madison darted a quick look at Joelle, carefully choosing her words so as not to upset the little girl.

"We'll agree to disagree. The horse has got to go. I'll ask around town to see if anyone knows who dropped the mare off. Otherwise, I'll find a new home for the horse. Just because it says she can't be sold; doesn't mean I can't find someone else in need of a horse for spiritual healing. Besides, what could a horse possibly do to help someone?"

"Perhaps you should read up on the legacy. Maybe the internet will have more information on the subject. But I don't think you should decide yet. It's not like you don't have a barn, and you said you used to love to ride. Maybe it's time you did again."

"No. Not anymore. I sold our horses for a reason, and nothing has changed." It also irritated him to no end that someone thought he needed help to get through his grief like he was some lost soul after his wife died. And so what if he was?

Joelle.

She was the reason it mattered.

The unwanted thought came out of nowhere, but it was a thought he couldn't ignore.

Chapter Six

♥

"Well, no matter what you decide to do with Star, she's yours for the time being." Madison moved closer and stroked the horse's mane, Joelle still firmly planted on her hip.

"Keep Joelle away from the horse. That's a new rule starting at once," Caleb said, taking his daughter from Madison and moving back to a safer distance.

"But Daddy, she's so pretty and I want to ride her," Joelle said, stretching out her arm toward the horse, her initial fear a thing of the past.

The regal white mare had an aura of calm that would draw people instantly. Combined with the scent of fresh hay in a barn, it brought back welcome memories of when he used to ride with Lauren. "She's too big for you, sweetheart," Caleb said, not giving in to her plea.

"But you could take me for a ride. You and Mommy used to ride, remember Daddy? And you took me with you. Just like the picture in my room."

Caleb shook his head. "Things have changed, and I don't ride anymore, so neither do you. It's dangerous. Something I wish I knew before I ever bought horses and stabled them here." His voice had grown tense and Madison sensed he was withdrawing into a dark place.

"Star is quite gentle, Caleb." Madison moved down and patted the horse's flank, and then back to hug her neck, proving her point.

"You've known the horse all of five minutes, don't assume you can judge her character. And either way, it doesn't matter. My decision is final. There'll be no riding."

"Not all horses spook easily, you know. And whether you want to hear it or not, Lauren wouldn't have wanted you to quit riding." Madison was venturing into unchartered territory and only slightly worried Caleb would go ballistic. She knew about the snake that caused the horse to rear up and unseat Lauren, but she also knew it was just an accident with a terrible ending. People ride horses every day, but with safe handling and trained horsemanship, accidents didn't happen often. And Lauren had been quite experienced, having ridden practically all her life.

"This is not a subject up for discussion," he snapped. "Perhaps you should take Joelle back to the house and let me figure out what I'm going to do to get rid of Star."

Madison moved to take Joelle and held out her arms. "It would be a mistake. The horse is a gift. A very endearing, well-thought-out gift meant to help heal wounds. Perhaps you should give her a shot. You might be surprised."

The deep grooves across his forehead intensified. If ears could smoke...they would be. It was time to retreat, but she wouldn't give up trying to make him understand this wasn't what Lauren would have wanted. For him or her daughter.

"The only thing that would surprise me is to figure out who would do such a thing. Everyone around here knows I don't ride."

"Perhaps it's a greater-good opportunity." Madison shot him a smile and left the barn without another word.

"Why won't daddy let me ride?" Joelle asked, her face scrunched up in disdain.

"As you know, your mother fell off a horse in a riding incident. She died and went to heaven. I think your dad is worried something will happen to you that he can't control. He loves you and is trying to keep you safe, sweetie."

Madison wanted more for Joelle, but it was important the little girl understood Caleb's protectiveness stemmed from love. Life happens, and sometimes not at all in the way we plan, and it hurts. Leaves us raw with emotion. But to retreat from the world and not live and enjoy every moment God gives us was a second tragedy. And by the looks of things, that's exactly what Caleb was trying to do.

"He tells me no to everything." Joelle's pout reflected her frustration. Madison vowed that while she was a nanny, her charge would do lots of fun things. As they walked back, Madison used the time to check out the house and pasture, loving the painted white wood siding and red roof that matched the barn. The fence bordered the long gravel drive and went as far as she could see. Caleb must have a lot of acreage, the pasture inviting with its open fields and trees in the distance. It was a shame he didn't use it anymore.

They moved onto the back porch, and Madison gazed back at the barn. Caleb was turning the horse out to pasture. He hadn't forgotten how to care for a horse, and compassion ran deep enough in his veins not to turn his back on the mare.

Caleb started their way...and oddly enough, so did Star. Every step of the way, the mare followed him along the fence line. Even more surprising was to see Caleb stop, speak to the horse, and then continue on his way.

Madison grinned, her cheeks to the point of hurting.

"Why is the horse following Daddy?" Joelle asked.

"Because she likes him. Horses connect with people in unusual ways and Star seems to be forging a bond with your dad." Whether Caleb liked it or not. Whoever had gifted the horse seemed to have done their homework well.

"Maybe Star senses how sad my Daddy is?"

"Maybe, honey." The words broke Madison's heart. Not only for Caleb but also for his daughter. She might only be turning six in the fall, but she was quite perceptive to the world around her. Even though it was a small world, it was filled with sadness.

"Maybe Star will like me too. I'm sad," Joelle said, her voice dropping so low that Madison barely heard the words.

"Because of your mom?" Madison asked, unsure how far to go down this road. What did she know about grief counseling?

Joelle nodded.

"Try not to be sad because your mom is always right here," Madison said, touching the region of Joelle's heart. "She would want you to be happy. Trust me."

"Really?"

"Absolutely," Madison confirmed, taking Joelle by the hand to head inside the house.

"And Daddy too?"

Madison nodded. "And your dad too."

Joelle was happy to play with her dolls while Madison set out to clean the place up a bit. He hadn't asked, but it was a simple thing to do. And it gave her a chance to check on Caleb. Madison peeked out the kitchen window and was more than a little surprised to see Caleb stroking the horse's neck. It was almost as though he were talking to Star, but that would be unbelievable.

It wasn't long before the back door opened and Caleb stepped inside.

"I see you and Star are getting along," Madison said, trying to figure out what was happening. Or more likely, hoping he had reconsidered.

Caleb shrugged and moved to get a glass of water. "I never said I hated horses. It's the riding part that's the problem."

"Well, you could have fooled me the way you wouldn't let Joelle within five feet of Star."

"That's because she's just a little girl and that's a big horse with big teeth and even bigger hooves on the end of some powerful legs."

"I see you've given this some thought," she teased.

"I mean it, Madison. Keep my daughter away from Star."

The man was far too serious and determined to get his way. Something Madison would have to work on while she was here. "Yes, boss."

Caleb finished the glass of water and put it in the dishwasher. "I've got to get to work on balancing the bank statements. I'll be in the dining room if you need me." He started toward the door of the kitchen, intent on leaving.

To the best of her knowledge, this hadn't been the plan. "*Umm*, the dining room? You're staying home? I thought you had to go to the store, and that's what this was all about. My job, I mean."

"At first, I want to get a sense of how you and Joelle get along while I'm still here. There's no reason I can't balance the bank statements at home. And if my uncle brings the ledger printouts tomorrow, I can focus on those while I'm here as well."

"Sounds like you don't trust me to do my job, so why hire me in the first place?" Madison asked.

Caleb shook his head. "I hired you because I can't keep a one hundred percent watch on Joelle and concentrate on the bookwork. I explained that when we set up this arrangement this morning."

He was right, but she thought he wanted to work at Bigsby's. This was fine too, but she hadn't planned on spending much time around Caleb.

There was still her heart to protect. And she knew the perfect solution. Busy work. "I see. Well, if you get in a jam, let me know. I can lend a hand while Joelle naps." Numbers always distracted her and would give her an escape from her own current troubles, instead of stewing on the issue.

"Why? Were you an accountant or a banker in the city? I'm assuming you weren't always a dog walker."

Was he trying to be funny? If he was, he was missing the mark because his comment was on the verge of condescending. "Nope. Fashion designer. However, it turned out I was nothing more than a glorified gopher with the design assistant title. It was more like a designer's personal assistant. Julia, the owner, didn't want me for my fashion skills, only my ability to handle her schedules and her financial affairs. She was a very private woman. It took me a few years to figure out that if I wanted to design clothes and not schedules, I needed to quit. It was either go after my dream or end up stuck in a dead-end job forever." She had already wasted five years in the woman's employ and still had no design experience to show for it. At least none that counted. Not that she didn't have plenty of her designs in her portfolio, but that's as far as she had got in her career.

"So, more than a pretty fashion designer?" Caleb said, unable to hide his smile.

The *pretty* part of his remark set her heart racing. "So, it would seem. The fashion designer part, anyway."

"You don't think you're pretty?" he challenged, suddenly serious.

Madison blushed. "Not really, and I don't care. I prefer brains over looks any day."

"Are you fishing for a compliment?" Caleb asked, his grin firmly back in place.

"Hardly." Madison moved away to rinse the dishes in the sink, preferring to avoid more conversation that centered on her.

Caleb moved off, and the conversation halted. Not that she didn't keep repeating it over and over in her head. He thought she was pretty.

The day passed, and Madison found lots to do to keep her busy, including playtime with Joelle. The little girl was a delight in every way.

Several times throughout the afternoon, she would spot Caleb watching them. He seemed more than a little stressed as he tapped the pen on the table, as though willing the numbers to fall into place. By the time she put Joelle down for a nap, she was determined to help him. It would beat sitting around and doing nothing since she had everything else under control.

Caleb looked up as she approached. "Joelle's sleeping and judging by the looks of the stack of statements in front of you, you haven't got very far."

He tossed the pen on the stack of papers and ran a hand across the back of his neck, massaging the corded muscles. "It's not like I kept track of expenses. I let everything go after Lauren died, letting things take care of themselves so I could take care of Joelle. In hindsight, I should have had more oversight. Something I'll fix, but first, I've got to get caught up."

"I couldn't agree with you more." Madison moved to stand behind him and peered over his shoulder. "Instead of starting with the oldest statements, why don't you start with the newest? It might be the easiest to remember and piece together the ins and outs of what you remember." This close, his cologne played with her senses, the woody musk as down to earth as the man.

Caleb sat back in his chair. "Sounds like a good idea. Thanks."

Sitting next to him, she pointed at the stack farthest from her, having noted the order he'd put them in. "Hand me the first one, and let's talk about the entries and make notes. There are few debits and credits to speak of," she said, reviewing the statement. "Let's start with the obvious...the deposits. I see five, and I'm assuming they're from the store."

"Yes. My uncle deposits them weekly. And I checked those first and none of them have gone astray in the past year. Fifty-two weeks and fifty-two deposits, some not exactly a week apart, but those correspond with holidays." Smart thinking on his part.

"That was a great idea to check those. This gives me another idea...since you're more focused on the store rather than your accounts, why don't we dig into those first? I can spot-check your debits along the way to make sure nothing is out of the ordinary." His financial problems had to have a reason. The trick was figuring out the trail the data could reveal. Numbers didn't lie. Not if they added up.

"Have at it," Caleb said, shoving the stack toward her. "And thanks. I'm not normally this irresponsible with finances. I promise."

"Good to know. That means when we get you straightened away, you'll be able to keep up without hiring someone to do it for you," she teased.

"*If* we get it straightened out."

"Ye of little faith." Madison laughed, pushing her hair off her face to see better.

She spent the next twenty minutes deep in thought, barely noticing when Caleb left the room and returned with a cup of coffee until he sat it in front of her, the chicory aroma wafting her way. "Thank you," she said, sitting back in her seat and savoring a sip.

"You're welcome. It's the least I could do seeing as you've taken over. Not that I'm complaining. When I hired you as a nanny, I didn't know I was getting a financial wiz as a bonus."

Another compliment. On the surface, Caleb had changed, his heart hardened by fate. But now and then, glimpses of the man she once knew showed up. A truly nice man with a big heart who once saw life with rose-colored glasses. "Hardly that, but I noticed a trend that bears digging a little deeper to find out why it's happening."

"And what's that?" he asked, standing behind her and leaning over to see what she was working on.

"It's not so much anything you would see on each statement, or pay attention to, but I set you up an Excel spreadsheet, and then played with it a bit. Look at this," she said, tilting the screen for him to see.

"What am I looking for?"

She pointed to one column. "There's a sort function that allows me to look at data in a multitude of ways. Week to week, some variations make it hard to see when you sort by date, but when you sort by monthly totals, the pattern is obvious. For the past year, the monthly deposits have been less and less. Which is why eventually, they stopped covering your expenses and you ended up with a negative cash flow." It wasn't much, but it was a start.

Caleb frowned. "But why? I mean, my uncle told me business is off since a new drugstore opened in Norwich, but this decrease in revenue is more than what I would expect from a little healthy competition."

"So, it's a trend, not the answer. A starting point, so to speak, but a good one because your debits have stayed consistent. The trick now is to figure out why your revenue is decreasing at a steady monthly rate." At least the afternoon wasn't a total loss, and they would have something to work on tomorrow.

"When my uncle delivers the ledgers, hopefully, we will find some answers. Fast. I can't continue to have less income at the rate of decrease you see. The emergency funds I'm using to get back up and running won't last long. I'm glad you offered to help. This might have taken days for me to see."

"Or weeks," she teased, turning away to hide her blush. The man had her heart doing flip-flops with his compliments.

"Maybe you have a bright future in accounting," Caleb said, never taking his eyes off her.

Madison shook her head. "No. My passion is fashion." Unfortunately, her passion for design wasn't paying the bills.

"I get you didn't like the job, but most people get a new job before they quit. And I'm sure it was an enormous culture shock coming back to Dover," he said, his voice tinged with curiosity as he sat down next to her.

It was the same thing she'd told herself many times, but the decision had felt right. Of course, that was before her car broke down. "It wasn't too bad seeing as I grew up here. And as to why so sudden...it was time I believed in myself. Mom had been after me to come for a visit, and the timing worked out to make us both happy. I've got several interviews lined up already, so it won't be long, and something will pan out. And then, who knows when I'll be able to come back to Dover again for a visit."

"Aren't there any jobs here in town?" he asked.

"Not in fashion. I could be a stock clerk at your store, but you've already got one," Madison teased.

Caleb chuckled. "True, and I'm not sure dressing mannequins is what you have in mind."

"Depends on whether it's my designs. Perhaps we could create a boutique corner in the store." Nonsensical talk, but a welcome relief after her head started spinning with numbers. They both needed the break.

"Doubt there would be much call for that around here." The flat tone of his voice dismissed her comment as though designer clothes were frivolous.

Madison shook her head, more than ready to defend her chosen career. "Laugh, but people need clothes...and women like to look nice. There's no harm in helping them find what works for their body shape and personal style."

"Glad I'm not a woman. Jeans and t-shirts are so much easier." Caleb grinned, restoring the easy camaraderie between them.

"They are until you wear designer jeans. You know, the kind that shows off your derriere." Madison blushed the minute the words slipped out. Seemed she was doing a lot of that around this man, proof she wasn't as immune to him as she had hoped.

Caleb frowned. "Not my thing."

"Maybe it should be." Since when did she add flirt to her list of character traits?

Chapter Seven

Caleb's uncle wasn't able to get the documents together for yesterday, but he promised to bring them by today. Instead, Caleb had spent the day trying to figure out who might have dropped Star off, but as of yet, he hadn't turned up any leads. He also spent some time learning more about Sundancer's Legacy. There were lots of stories where recipients gave high praise for the gift of love that exceeded all expectations. Not once did he find a story of someone returning a horse, or that claimed peace and happiness were but an illusion for fools.

Some folks claimed it was a magical healing power, but others described it more as a healing that came from caring about something else. The ability to open oneself up to a connection requiring more than a surface reflection of what existed in someone's heart. It came from learning to love again. Horses were good judges of people. And for him, that meant Sundancer's Star. The more tales he read, the less inclined he felt towards giving the beautiful mare away. And he had to admit, his focus on Star's upkeep had allowed him to bond with her. It was as though he were forging a connection with the past, instead of wallowing in it.

He couldn't imagine someone understanding his deep-rooted need for help that he tried to ignore. Didn't want to admit it if he was being honest. There were certainly times Caleb had wondered how long life could continue this way. Until now, it had been easier not to fight his way out of the darkness. Not to mention, when Joelle went to preschool, he knew things would change dramatically. Their lives would no longer be just the two of them.

Horses had regular feeding and grooming schedules and Caleb was resigned to take Joelle with him each morning before Madison arrived. She skipped alongside him, holding his hand.

"Daddy, I want to pet the horsey, okay?"

"We will see, sweetheart. Star is pretty big, and I worry you'll get hurt."

"Frieda was big, and she didn't hurt me." She spoke like a staunch champion for her cause.

"Horses are even bigger and more powerful, trust me."

"Was the horse bad that made mommy die?" The question took Caleb by surprise. It's not as if she had been old enough at the time to understand. A simmering anger hovered near the surface, threatening to overcome him as the accident replayed in his head. The same way it had done so many times over the past year and a half. The horse reared up as a snake startled Joker, Lauren's prized gelding. She always said Joker was just like her...a free spirit.

When Lauren had come out of the saddle and landed wrong on the tree, his wife had died in his arms leaving a hole the size of Texas in his heart. In a split second his life had changed, and happiness seemed far too elusive. Joy always seemed just out of reach, and each day had been difficult to carry on. Caring and loving Joelle had been the only thing to see him through the darkest of days. After selling all the horses, he thought it would bring him peace.

Not so.

"Daddy?" his daughter asked again, still waiting for an answer.

As much as he wanted to blame the horse, he couldn't do it. "No. Your mother loved Joker, and the two had been together for years. It was an unfortunate accident." A preventable one if he had only cut the tree away after it had fallen in the path.

"Where's Joker now?"

"Some people in another town bought him when I sold the horses."

"I would love to have mommy's horse. Then I could ride anytime I wanted, and it would be like riding with mommy." In his haste to sell the horses, not once had he considered the possibility his daughter would want the horse someday. Had he done the wrong thing selling Joker? At the time, selling Joker had seemed like the right thing to do.

They entered the barn, the fresh aroma of manure and hay greeting him like an old friend. Star whinnied and shook her head, pleased to see him. Or more than likely, knowing her breakfast had arrived. Caleb pulled an apple from his pocket and cut it up, then held it out in the palm of his hand for Star.

"Can I feed her?" Joelle asked.

"I've only got the one apple and I'm sure you don't want to risk Star biting your hand. Why don't you watch me this time?" Caleb chuckled. When Star finished all the pieces, Caleb stroked her long neck. "Good girl. You're in a strange place and probably wondering why, aren't you?"

"Why did someone give her to you?"

"I'm not sure. Maybe they thought we would make a good pair." It was more than that, no matter how smart or advanced Joelle was for her age, she wouldn't understand the meaning of the Legacy and the whys of someone who was chosen to receive such a precious gift. It would also require him to admit his grief to Joelle, something he would never do. She had more than enough to deal with losing her mother without him heaping onto the pile.

"So, are we going to keep her?" she asked.

He considered the options. "I don't know. There's so much going on and the timing doesn't seem right."

Joelle took a step closer. "But you always tell me to say thank you when I get a gift and to be g...gr...what's that word?"

"Grateful." Caleb shook his head. His daughter certainly had a way of bringing his words full circle.

"Pick me up so I can pet her, please," his daughter pleaded, moving to stand next to him.

There was no sense fighting the inevitable. Better to teach her how to touch a horse and how to respect one, than to have her learn the wrong way. It would seem his daughter would have the same attraction to horses that her mother did. He picked Joelle up and settled her on his hip for support. "Let her smell your hand and move slowly so as not to startle her."

"I thought she would be soft, but her hair is prickly." Joelle giggled.

"Be extra gentle until she trusts you. You know the same way you like it when I rub your hair. It's soothing."

"I like that. Especially after I take out my ponytail. Do ponies wear ponytail bands in their long fur?"

Caleb held up a section of the long white hair for Joelle to feel the course texture. "That's called a mane, and no, not normally. Only sometimes if someone shows them."

Joelle scrunched up her nose as she reached out to touch the side of Star's face. "Shows them what?"

"Like in a dog show...only for horses." Caleb loved Joelle's curiosity. It was a good sign she would always thirst for knowledge.

Joelle nodded. "Ohhh, like we see on TV."

Star nuzzled Caleb's shoulder, looking for him to pay some attention to her. He smiled and patted the mare, unable to resist. Caleb set Joelle on the ground. "Stay back while I get her fresh feed and water. Then we can run up to the house to meet Madison and I'll come back to clean her stall and turn her out to pasture."

"Can I come with you when you do?"

"We'll see. That depends on Madison since she's your nanny." Joelle would slow things down and the idea was to make more time so that he could work on the ledgers today. The sound of a car door shutting alerted him Madison must have arrived.

Early...a trait he always liked. "Madison's here. Let's go."

"Yay. I like Miss Madison."

Hand in hand, they rounded the front of the house, only to discover the visitor wasn't Madison. "Uncle Bill, it's great to see you. I'm guessing you have the ledgers?" he asked, more than ready to move to stage two of trying to find out where everything had gone off course.

"Sure do," he said, holding up a stack of pages held together with a giant clasp. "I don't think this is a case of anything more than the competition stealing away some of our clientele, but have at it."

"Thanks. I just need to be more actively involved. If things are this bad, I may have to let Tommy go...and possibly even you if I expect to keep the place afloat." He was hoping it wouldn't come to that, but he would do everything in his power to save the store.

Uncle Bill frowned. "Surely it can't be that bad. I mean, you're making money every week."

He didn't want to get into this right here and now, not with Joelle listening. "Dwindling balances are a huge problem when it comes to paying bills."

"Tommy makes the deposits every week, but I trust him. I know he's acting a little edgy lately, but I think his home life is stressing him out. He takes care of his family, you know." Bill shrugged as though perplexed by the whole situation.

"I had no idea. That's a lot on his shoulders," Caleb said, taking the sheath of papers from his uncle. Tommy had a motive for mischief, which was something to consider.

Madison pulled up to the front of the house and slid out of the car.

Caleb let go of Joelle's hand and she ran to meet her nanny. "Miss Madison, you're here. I missed you." His daughter took Madison by the hand and led her toward them.

"I missed you too, sweetheart. I've got some fun planned for today."

"Yay," Joelle said, her answering smile a welcome sight.

"Good morning, Madison. You're just in time to meet my Uncle Bill."

"It's nice to meet you. Caleb has nothing but good things to say about you, and I know you've been a big help to him."

They shook hands. "I do what I can, but it's not enough," Uncle Bill said, slightly on the defensive.

Caleb hated that his uncle felt responsible for anything happening at the store. If he hadn't pushed his responsibility for Bigsby's off on him, this might not have been a problem. Either that or it would have happened anyway...if the problem was the new store in the next town over.

"We'll get through this. We must. My parents entrusted me with Bigsby's when they went off on the adventure of a lifetime. And even though they're gone now, I don't want to let them down. I know they're watching over me from heaven, and with any luck, I can figure out how to save the place."

At the mention of his parents, his uncle had grown quiet, his face void of expression. Perhaps the memory of losing his sister still had the power to hurt his uncle. The same way it hurt Caleb. And much the same way he hurt losing Lauren.

"And I'm helping Caleb go over the books, which would seem to be even more of a blessing to him than I originally thought given the antiquated system he has in place," she teased, glancing at the stack of papers in his hand.

"At least there is a system. It was good enough for my dad," Caleb said, trying to defend his lack of modernization.

"Times have changed, and it's a lot easier to figure out mistakes when the computer systems are running data checks," Madison said.

"You're an accountant?" his uncle asked.

Madison shrugged, lobbing her head from side to side as though unsure how to answer.

"Yes, and no. I was a glorified gopher assistant to my last boss, who required me to handle her finances," she explained.

Uncle Bill nodded; lines of tension firmly etched on his forehead. Either that or they were from years of playing golf in the sun. "I see. Guess some experience is better than Caleb's lack of it."

"Time will tell." Madison laughed.

His uncle glanced at his watch. "I've got to run. Let me know if you find anything," Uncle Bill said, waving a hand as he headed for his truck.

"What do you two have planned today?" Caleb asked.

"We're going to make the pipe animals, since we didn't get to it yesterday. You know...with the pipe cleaners you were highly suspicious of," Madison teased.

"I want to make a pink elephant," Joelle declared, taking Madison by the hand. "Come on," she said, pulling her nanny toward the house. It would seem his daughter had all but forgotten her earlier request to help with Star once Madison arrived.

"I'll be down at the barn taking care of Star, and then I'll be in the dining room if you need me. Digging into data...you know, the boring stuff."

"Not to mention it gives you a better way to keep an eye on us." Madison shot him a wink. "Yes, I can tell. You're not very subtle...but I don't mind."

Busted. "It's not..."

"Sure, it is." Madison's laughter trickled his way until the screen door closed behind her.

Caleb was left standing there, more than a little mortified at having been caught out. He hadn't thought he was being obvious, but clearly, he was wrong.

Thirty minutes later, he had accomplished next to nothing. The sound of laughter in the kitchen caught his attention, as well as the image of watching Joelle and Madison creating their pipe animals. The two were having loads of fun, something he wanted to be doing with his daughter. But lately, Joelle found everything they did boring, as though she were itching to do more, but not knowing what. And Caleb didn't have a clue how to entertain a child her age...safely. The older a child got, the more that was out there that could trip them up.

Tossing his pen on the table, he stood and crossed the room to join them. "Sounds like fun in here. Don't tell me the animals are coming to life?"

"No silly, Daddy. It's just us making animal noises." Joelle held up her elephant and made a loud trumpet sound. Madison caught his gaze and hid her laugh. Joelle sounded more like a horse whinnying, but no one cared. "Your turn, Miss Madison," Joelle said.

"*Hmmm*. Well, since I made a lion...rooooaarr," she said, moving the lion toward Joelle. "I'm King of the Jungle," Madison added in a deep voice.

Caleb grinned. "I hate that I'm missing all the fun."

"You can make a pipe animal too. It's easy, Daddy."

"What should I make? Maybe a dog?" Caleb was trying to think of something easy and that Joelle would like as a gift when he was done. That is if he had more talent for making pipe animals than he did at balancing the books. But this would be way more fun.

"I think you should make Star," Joelle said, her blue eyes lit with excitement at the idea.

"I thought this was animals?" Caleb teased.

"Star's an animal. She's a horse…even I know that," Joelle said, handing him a white pipe cleaner.

"Star it is." Of course, he'd known what his daughter meant, but where was the fun in not doing a play on the words for a little humor? He tried to get a sense of what to do by checking out the completed pipe animals while Madison and Joelle worked on new ones.

"You're doing great. You just need the glue to tack on some eyes and some paint to make the hooves black," Madison said, handing him a strip of small plastic containers. The back of his hand caught the edge of the strip, turning it up on end, black paint coming out of the open tub and landing on the sleeve of Madison's blue blouse.

"I'm so sorry," he exclaimed as she stepped back, looking down in horror at the mess he was making. He reached out and tried to wipe off the paint.

"Stop, you're making it worse," Madison said, moving to the sink. "It will be okay, I promise."

"Daddy made a big mess," Joelle said, one hand over her mouth as she laughed, Madison joining in.

He was the only one who saw no humor in ruining Madison's clothes. Even though it was in fact, how they met. Madison getting Caleb and his daughter covered in mud. "It's such a beautiful blouse and I've ruined it. Hopefully, you'll let me pay for the mistake or maybe I can buy you another one to replace it."

Madison's smile grew wider. "That would be difficult to do."

"Why is that?" he asked.

Madison leveled him with a thoughtful gaze, an eyebrow quirked upward slightly. "It's one of a kind."

Ouch. Caleb knew nothing about fashion, but he understood *one of a kind*. It usually came with a hefty price tag. The royal blue blouse with its open shoulder keyholes, and delicate lace trim that framed the V-neck and trailed down the sleeves, all but shouted expensive. "I'm truly sorry. Just tell me how much and I'll add it to your paycheck." Yes, he needed to be careful with his money now, but it was only right he paid for something he destroyed. Even if it was an accident.

"As much as I'd loved the bonus, it won't be necessary as I didn't pay for the blouse…well, other than my time and material. It's one of my designs," Madison said.

"Really? It's lovely." Her words had taken him by surprise, not because he knew the first thing about fashion, but because he knew high quality and pretty. And he had noticed the shade of royal blue matched her eyes perfectly when she'd first arrived this morning. And that the soft material fell gracefully to fit her curves. It was also a thought he shoved aside, helped, of course, knowing his uncle had been present. "Perhaps I could still pay you something?" he offered, at a loss for what else to do.

"Let's just call us even since Freida got you all muddy and you wouldn't accept my help. Besides, look," she said, holding up her arm and the sleeve for his inspection. "All gone."

Caleb was shocked, but mostly relieved. "Wow. You must have some magical powers to get a black stain out."

Madison grinned. "Nope. It's called washable paint," she teased. "Time to finish our animals and then I've got to make lunch."

"Washable paint. Who knew? But I'm glad. I should get back to work on the books. I've made enough of a mess for one afternoon." His brief break had been disastrous, but he had enjoyed it while it lasted. Just a little something to take his mind off the serious side of life.

"I'll finish making Star. I'm going to make her beautiful. She'll be perfect for you, Daddy."

"Thank you, sweetheart." Star was perfect...just not perfect for him. And another reason for him to get back to work. Having fun with Madison and his daughter didn't seem right. It should have been Lauren and his daughter, but that was impossible considering God had called Lauren home.

Chapter Eight

♥

Joelle was busy playing school with her dolls and failed to notice Caleb's arrival, but Madison stood and crossed the room, closing the distance between them. "You look like a man on a mission. What's up?"

"I've got to run to the store if you think you'll be all right here? His gaze drifted toward Joelle. It would be the first time leaving them alone, proof he was headed in the right direction. Time away from his normal routine would do him good, even if for nothing more than to rebuild his confidence in life.

Madison nodded. "Absolutely. We've got lots to keep us busy. Take your time. Maybe you should stop at the diner and grab a coffee. Talk to folks."

"The store will be enough this go round. You're sure about this, right?" Caleb hesitated by the front door; indecision etched on his face. How would he ever let his daughter go to kindergarten if he didn't start working on trusting others to care for his daughter?

"Go. That's an order," she said, laughing at him as she opened the door and gave him a gentle shove. "Joelle won't even notice you left. It's the first day of doll school and she's the teacher, so she has to give the students her utmost attention." Madison grinned.

"Thanks. I think. It's not saying much if she doesn't notice I'm gone." Caleb frowned, but he stepped off the porch.

"It's what you want to happen, whether you understand or not at this point. You can't keep your daughter safe by hiding her under the cocoon of your watchful gaze. You teach her to be safe...and make good choices. That's parenting."

"I hope you're right."

"I am. Now go." Madison stepped back inside and closed the door, deciding for him. She did, however, peek through the curtains just to make sure he left. This would be good for both Caleb and Joelle, his obsession with keeping her safe not healthy for either of them.

Madison sat on the floor with Joelle, joining in the fun and games. Getting paid to play was a novelty and she intended to enjoy every second.

"This is Susan, and this is Sally. *Hmmm*," she added, a frown marring her expression. "Or this is Sally, and this is Susan. I'm not a good teacher cause I can't remember their names."

"That's not true. With so many kids' names to remember every year, it's difficult to keep them straight, especially when twins are involved."

"Twins?"

"When two kids look the same and are born at the same time from the same mommy. They're called triplets when there's three babies." Madison grinned.

Joelle brightened. "Maybe daddy can get me another baby and then I'll have triplets. When I go to school, I hope the teacher knows my name."

Joelle was such a sweet child, and Madison couldn't help falling in love with the little girl. Precocious yet innocent. "You have a very unusual name and you're a bright young lady, so I'm sure the teacher will get to know you quickly."

"Tell me about school. I see kids on TV learning fun things, and sometimes when daddy and me drive past the school, the kids are outside playing. I want to play with them, but daddy says I have to wait until kindergarten."

"Which isn't that far off, sweetheart. Your dad tells me you've got a birthday coming in November."

"I'm going to be six," Joelle said, holding up six fingers. "I can't wait to go to school."

"That's so cool. Maybe your dad will let me take you shopping for school clothes and a bookbag and supplies. That would give us a chance to get out of the house, rain or shine." Not that kindergartners needed much, but still...there had to be neat things they could pick up to make it special.

"I want a book bag with a princess on it," Joelle said, hiding a yawn.

"Then that's what you'll get. Your first bookbag is super special. I'll ask your dad when he gets home, but for now, it looks like it's nap time," Madison said, standing up and holding out her hand to Joelle.

"Do I have to? Naps are for babies," Joelle whined, lending proof of the need for sleep.

Cranky children needed nothing more than a nap to recover their sweet spirits. Not that she'd used that word with Joelle. "Tired young children take naps. It's always been that way."

"Okay. I am a little sleepy. Will you tuck me in?" she asked, rubbing her eyes.

"Sure thing." Madison picked Joelle up and carried her to the bathroom and sat her down. "Go potty and then I'll get you all snug as a bug in a rug."

Joelle giggled. "I'm not a bug."

"No, but you're cute as a bug."

"Not a spider, though, right?" Joelle asked, her face scrunched in displeasure.

Madison shook her head. "No, something special, like a butterfly."

Joelle's eyes lit up, her soft smile adorable. "I like butterflies." Satisfied, she went into the bathroom. Minutes later, the toilet flushed, and the sink water ran before Joelle met her back in the hall. Caleb might be overly protective, but the man was a good father, and teaching Joelle basic life protocol wasn't one of his shortcomings.

They went into the princess' bedroom and Madison tucked Joelle in. "Sweet dreams," she said, dropping a kiss on Joelle's forehead before making sure the blankets were snug all around her.

"I like having you here." The words flooded Madison's heart with a wealth of feelings, her love blossoming for the child.

She would need to guard her heart, or she'd never want to leave. Of course, Joelle's handsome father and her old feelings that were coming to life weren't helping either. "Good, because I like being here."

Madison headed down the hall and sat down on the sofa with a glass of iced tea. And in less than ten minutes, she was bored. Not one to sit around, she headed for the dining room table and looked over the ledger statements. One by one, she jotted down notes, filled out hand-written charts, and extracted key data to get a better picture of what was going on at the store. Caleb hadn't said why he was going there, but perhaps it was to do the same thing but from a more hands-on approach.

Once she transferred all the basic data onto the chart, she moved to the couch, pen in hand. Looking for patterns or unusual entries, she circled and checked off the columns. Glancing at her watch, she couldn't believe an hour and a half had passed by so quickly. Joelle would wake up soon, and she fully expected Caleb home at any time. She was surprised he was still gone. It was rewarding to know he trusted her with his daughter. Not that she expected it to mean anything more than it probably was...a case of Lauren's friend would be a *better-than-most* option.

Madison turned her attention back to the columns of figures. Eighteen months of data and the one thing that stood out the most were consistent sales. Slight changes, yes, but all that could be explained with seasonality. Nothing significant, which would mean Caleb's uncle was wrong. Sales didn't drop because of the new store in Norwich. Locals shopped locally.

And if sales were consistent and income was lower, that only left one problematic area. Expenses. Actually, two areas...the other being deposits. But that was easy enough to match off what was deposited and what was net profit, and she doubted young Tommy, who made the deposits, would ever do anything illegal. He seemed like a good kid, and Madison was all about trusting her instincts. It was a small step forward, but the good news was that they could now focus their attention on the right area...expenses.

As if on cue, Joelle entered the living room, rubbing her eyes, just as Caleb walked through the front door.

"How's my little princess?" he asked, beaming when his gaze landed on her.

Dragging her blankie, she moved to sit next to Madison. "Not sleepy anymore. Guess Miss Madison was right 'cause I went right to sleep."

"I'm glad to hear it. Did you two have fun today?" Caleb asked.

"We played dolly school, and Madison, I mean Miss Madison, got right down on the floor and played with me. It was so much fun." Joelle's sunny smile was firmly back in place.

Madison took her by the hand and squeezed lightly, sharing in the assessment. "Sweetheart, I'm glad you enjoyed our afternoon, but please, call me Madison. It's more friendly, and I'd like you to think of us as friends.

"Okay. Did you hear that, Daddy? I have a new friend."

Caleb scooped his daughter into his arms and gave her a big hug. "I'm glad you had fun while

I was at the store. Daddy was working and didn't figure anything out." He turned his gaze to Madison. "I thought maybe something would occur to me, but mostly, I helped with customers. Lots of customers."

It was the same thing Madison had figured out using the data provided. "Which brings me to what I need to tell you. While you were gone and Joelle was sleeping, I was going over the ledgers, and guess what I found?" She couldn't keep the excitement from her voice.

"You figured out the problem? Really? That would be incredible," Caleb said, the dimples on his chin prominent with a broad smile.

Madison shook her head. "Not so fast. I wish it were that easy, but I analyzed the sales numbers and trends and the problem isn't declining business. Your uncle is wrong."

"Thank goodness for that. But what is it then?" Caleb asked.

"Well...if sales are consistent and bottom-line income is dropping, that only leaves an expense problem or a deposit problem. The deposits are easily verified, and I doubt Tommy would mess with those. I think we need to review all the expenses and see what's changed. The numbers could tell a story if someone knew what they were looking for."

"Makes sense. What do we need to move this forward?"

Madison noticed his use of the word "we" and couldn't help the surge of excitement that rippled down her spine. He was letting her into his inner circle of trusted friends, and it felt right. "We need the actual inventory ledgers and the receipts that go with them. It's a little more in-depth of a process, but the answer to the problem must be there."

"Then that's where we will look. Thank you for doing this. Truly." Caleb's gaze never left hers, neither of them saying a word. It was almost like a connection of sorts. An understanding.

Either that or she was seeing far more into his gratitude because she wanted to see more.

Chapter Nine

❤

Going to the store alone felt off at first, but gradually he stopped worrying about Joelle, knowing Madison was watching her. Lauren would have approved of his decision without question. And to prove to himself he could stay away, he opted to stay longer, hoping to find something useful and solve the store's financial woes.

The only problem solving it would seem had been done right here at home. Madison was more than a little amazing. "I've got to head to the barn and take care of Star. Anyone care to join me?" Caleb asked, not ready to let go of the camaraderie between them.

"I do. I do," Joelle said, suddenly wide-eyed and smiling, and jumping up and down.

"I second her two votes," Madison added.

Caleb held hands with his daughter as they all headed out the door. "I figured you wouldn't turn down the treat of visiting the barn." Truth be told, he enjoyed his visits to see Star, using the opportunity to talk to the horse, even knowing she wouldn't answer. Although Star had a few ways of making him aware of her agreement, or disagreement, as sometimes happened.

"Most people wouldn't consider a barn visit a treat," Madison teased as she stepped off the porch.

"True, but you and Joelle aren't most people." Caleb winked. He swung his daughter up into his arms and they started toward the barn.

Caleb pulled open the heavy wooden doors, noting a new squeak he needed to fix. The familiar scent of horse, hay, and manure assailed him, like an old friend. Star greeted them with a whinny as they drew near, signaling her appreciation at having company. As always, the mare nuzzled his arm, forcing him to not only acknowledge her, but to stroke her neck. And of course, talk to her. Even with the others around, he found it easy to do, not at all embarrassed in front of Madison or his daughter. "Good girl. Bet you're ready for some exercise."

Joelle reached out to pet the horse, gently the way he had shown her. "Are you going to ride the horse, Daddy?" she asked, her eyes twinkling with delight.

"No, sweetheart. I don't ride anymore. I'll turn Star out in the pasture so she can go for a run." Somewhere deep inside, the desire to ride sizzled to the surface, but he couldn't bring himself to change his decision.

Joelle cupped his head with her two hands, turning his face toward her. "But why don't you want to ride, Daddy? I want to ride."

Caleb shook his head. "I'm sorry, I just don't." He wasn't about to explain it to his daughter. Riding had always been a passion of his, but now, the very thought brought no joy. Only memories of Lauren. "Not everything can be explained, but since Madison tells me you've been good today, I'll teach you to brush her coat. She loves being groomed."

"Okay. Are we going to give her a bath?"

"Not today." Caleb was pleased Joelle didn't press the subject and was more than willing to let her take a bigger role in helping with the process. He moved to the table where he had laid some of the tack. "This is a curry brush," Caleb said, picking up the coarsely bristled brush. "She needs a good brushing and we'll be sure to comb her mane. Make her look all nice and pretty for her walk."

"I see how it is. You brought us here to work," Madison teased.

Caleb chuckled. "Ah, but it's not work if it's fun."

"Show me how to do it, Daddy. I want to have fun," Joelle said, taking the brush from him.

Caleb and Madison exchanged an all-knowing look. Getting a kid to see work as fun was half the battle. The other half was keeping it that way. "Here, like this," he said, taking her hand and guiding the strokes, starting at the neck, and moving down the flanks. "Not too hard so that it hurts, but enough pressure to make it feel good and loosen any dirt and dust that accumulates." Caleb would be sure to add a few extra strokes of his own knowing Joelle's touch would be super soft.

Madison held Star's halter while he worked with Joelle. She stroked Star's nose and spoke to her in a gentle voice. The horse loved all the attention and swished her tail a few times to show it. It would seem Madison also had a way with horses, something Caleb couldn't fail to appreciate.

"How do you know so much about horses?" he asked.

"Growing up, I used to hang out in the stables at the end of our street. The owners taught me to ride and in exchange, I worked in the barn and stables, learning about their care. It was a win-win situation. Unfortunately, we moved into town after my dad passed away and then I didn't have a way to get out there since mom worked. But once you learn, the knowledge and the love of horses never goes away," she said, her hand stopping mid-stroke as she caught his gaze, a wealth of meaning in her words.

"Perhaps you're right, but sometimes love simply isn't enough." It hadn't been enough to keep his wife alive. And it wasn't enough to keep him riding. But Madison was right, his love for horses still lived deep inside. And Star knew it. "Time to turn her out into the pasture while I muck out her stall."

"Okay. I'll head inside and get dinner started. Joelle, why don't you come with me?" Madison asked, reaching for his daughter.

"Can I help you cook dinner?" Joelle asked, practically leaping from his arms to go with Madison. The nanny had certainly scored a big hit with his daughter.

"Certainly. You're always a big help in the kitchen." Madison was being too kind.

Caleb knew Joelle was no such thing, always making bigger messes. But Madison had the patience of a saint...or someone who would make a great mom one day.

After they left, Caleb pulled out the apple he'd snagged from the refrigerator. Using his pocketknife, he sliced it up, offering it as a treat to Star. Chance, his old horse loved apples, and a special bond had been formed by the nightly ritual. It would seem Star, too, had a penchant for Red Delicious apples.

The spaghetti dinner had been a big hit with both Joelle and Caleb. It was one of those go-to meals that never went astray and one Madison relied on often. And plenty of sauce meant easy-to-fix meals with fresh pasta lickety-split quick. "Do you want me to stay and look over the ledgers some more tonight? I don't have anything else I need to do, so I don't mind."

Caleb shook his head. "I wouldn't want to impose. You've done so much extra already, and I'm sure I'm taking you out of circulation."

Madison grinned. "I don't mind, honestly. Other than visiting with my mother, I don't go out much. I thrive on challenges. Ask my mom if you don't believe me."

"Say yes, Daddy. I want Madison to stay," Joelle said, her words sending another positive tug of emotion to Madison's heart.

"I guess I'm outnumbered. I can put a movie on for Joelle and if you're positive you don't mind, we can go over the inventory sheets I picked up from the store while you were cooking dinner."

No one could resist the child's sweetness, including her father. "Sounds like a plan. So how did it go with Star?" Madison asked.

"Got everything done and then some. I'm still trying to figure out why she follows me around, but it's cute. Not something I've experienced with a horse before."

"Maybe it's the Legacy. Her power to connect and heal, if it's to be believed, would be miraculous. Talk about a special gift," Madison said, pointing out what Caleb already knew, but still hadn't quite accepted.

"But not one I needed," he countered.

"That remains to be seen. Star has singled you out, that much is undeniable, but what happens next, we can only wait and see." She wasn't letting him off the hook easily.

Caleb shrugged. "If I find a new home for Star, there won't be a next. So don't go getting too attached."

"I think she's beautiful and a nice addition to your family." Madison didn't want to point out the obvious, but perhaps the horse sensed Caleb's deep internalized grief and the mare looked to draw him out of the dark place he'd retreated to. Madison had done her research on the Legacy and fully believed Star's previous owner had chosen well. Caleb needed to reconnect with life and the living and perhaps tapping into something he once loved to do...riding horses would be the perfect way to spur the change. She wouldn't press the issue, letting God take control and use Star if that was the plan. Already, Caleb was making progress, his actions today proving how far he'd come to trusting her and spending time with her by choice.

Madison sat down at the table and sorted through the inventory sheets, trying to get a sense of how they were laid out and what data she would find. By the time she had them arranged in order, Caleb returned.

"Joelle picked Cinderella. It's one of her favorites. She'll be content for the next ninety minutes," Caleb said, settling in the chair next to her.

"Great. I've sorted through everything and arranged the inventory into stacks by each week, and then a monthly summary stack. Start with July of last year, comparing week-to-week entries to see if anything jumps out at you. I'll start from January to June and do the same. Highlight large increases in yellow and then we can step back and compare the data. If in doubt what's considered large, circle it anyway." Madison was ready to tackle this project and having two of them going over the data should make it quick work. The problem she saw in her plan was that once they found the problem, Caleb wouldn't need her anymore. And she loved spending time with them.

"I like your take-charge attitude. Having your help is awesome because it forces me to stay focused. Wouldn't want the boss to catch me slacking," he teased.

"Well, since I'm the employee, there's no chance of that. Like I said, I enjoy the challenge, not that I wouldn't rather be applying my skills creatively instead of mathematically, but this pays the bills." Luckily, she had an aptitude for both.

"Except I hired you to watch Joelle. You could be watching Cinderella, but you voluntarily gave that up for this." He gestured toward the stacks of papers spread out on the table.

"And miss all this fun? No way. Now quit stalling. Ninety minutes will go quickly."

"I'm on it," Caleb said, picking up the first four weeks of inventory sheets arranged neatly in front of where he was sitting.

The man liked to tap his marker on the table as he reviewed the ledgers, the sound somewhat distracting. And cute. Sneaking a peek at him as he worked, his mouth was drawn tight as he studied the figures. There were a few highlighted areas, but not many, which were good and bad. Good, there were no discrepancies. Bad they were no closer to figuring out the problem.

Madison continued to review her stacks, making quick work of the inventory sheets. There were a few entries that had steady increases, perhaps relative to the economy, but one jumped out at her. The BOGOP company expenses kept creeping up higher at an alarming rate, while most of the inventory remained steady. "Let me see what you have so far. I may have found something," Madison said.

"What is it?" Caleb had only gone through a few months by the time she'd finished her stacks, but he stopped, more than a little interested in seeing what she'd found.

"There's a company called BOGOP whose costs have risen at an alarming rate. Have you seen anything about them on your end?"

"BOGOP only just started showing up on my accounts, so I figured it was a seasonal thing. Am I missing something?" he asked.

A quick scan confirmed Caleb's assessment. It would seem the relationship with BOGOP only started in March. "It helps that I'm a little more well-versed in comparing the data. But in looking over what you've done so far, I see the jump to July and moving forward as significant. While you finish those up, I want to do some quick figures based on monthly totals."

"Have at it." Caleb grinned. "I've not heard of the company, so it must be someone my uncle started using."

Madison didn't like what she was seeing. Month after month, the increase was a steady pattern. Jotting down some notes on her tablet, she added up the increases, circling her last figure. "I think this may be your problem. Look," she said, pointing at the tablet. "The account started off spending hundreds of dollars a month in March. Each month, the expense got higher, and by the end of last year it was almost a thousand dollars a month."

Caleb nodded and let out a heavy sigh. "It's an issue, but it still doesn't explain the shortages I'm facing now."

"That's because you haven't seen this year's numbers on BOGOP. Look at this," she said.

Caleb stood and moved to stand behind Madison as she spread out the last six months of monthly summaries for this year. "What am I looking for?"

Madison pointed to her tablet and the chart she'd drawn. "Starting in February, the increases grew at a faster rate. To the tune of over ten thousand dollars in the last five months."

Caleb drew in a deep breath and shook his head. "That's almost in line with the shortages I've calculated in my account. I don't get it. What could my uncle possibly be buying that keeps getting more expensive, and why wouldn't he find another supplier?"

"That's what you need to find out. Call him. Find out what the BOGOP company sells and get his take on the situation. He is the manager, after all, and should fully expect questions given the situation."

Caleb frowned. "I don't want to upset him or make him think he's done something wrong. He's family and I trust him."

She reached out and grabbed his hand to stop him from walking away. "It's either that or lose the store. Take your pick." Madison wanted to deal with the issue head on.

"Fine." He pulled his phone from his pocket and pressed a few buttons. It wasn't long before the two men were exchanging greetings, the corded muscles of his neck rippling with tension.

"Hey, Uncle Bill. We've been going over some accounts payable ledgers, and Madison has found something we need to discuss. We've discovered an issue with one account and I'm hoping you can shed some light for us."

Madison could hear Bill talking but couldn't make out the words. She tried to gauge the conversation using Caleb's facial expressions and was rewarded with a sudden smile as he pressed the speakerphone button.

"What seems to be the problem? You know I feel terrible about the store revenue declining and I've tried to increase sales. If there's anything I can do, just say the word," Bill offered.

"I know you have tried to help, and I'm sure this isn't your fault. What can you tell me about the BOGOP company? The capital expense with them seems out of line, but then I don't even know what you are ordering from them. There's no description of goods."

"Oh, that's a marketing company I started doing business with. They offer Buy One, Get One deals we can sell to our customers. I figure we needed to draw people into the store and keep them shopping here instead of going to the new store. I thought it was working." Madison believed the man, as he seemed genuinely distressed.

Caleb ran a hand through his hair and nodded. "I see. It makes sense, but unfortunately, it's not working. We need to stop doing business with BOGOP immediately. There has to be a better way to drum up business. The account is costing us exorbitant sums of money we can't afford based on revenue."

"I'm sorry. I should have tracked it better. I'll shut it down at once. Hopefully, it's not too late to salvage things," Bill said.

"We'll be fine if we get that in line. I feel sure of it," Caleb said, letting out another deep breath.

Madison stood, excited they had solved the problem. Caleb wouldn't lose the store...and even if it meant she would be out of a job, it was all good. Caleb and Joelle had become special to her in just a few short days.

"Thanks for the vote of confidence, Caleb," Bill said, sounding more than a little relieved.

"No problem. Family must stick together. Have a good night."

"You do the same," Bill said before the call was disconnected.

Madison clapped her hands, a wide smile at the ready. "Sounds like we figured it out."

"More like you did, but yes, I agree. Problem solved. Thank you so much for your help," Caleb said, his hand coming up toward her face, almost as though it had a will of its own. Touching her cheek, his thumb caressed her face softly. It was as though time had stopped between them.

His gaze held her with an intensity she couldn't look away from. Was he going to kiss her? No way. It surely had to be a figment of her imagination.

Madison swallowed hard as Caleb lowered his head. This was no figment. Caleb Duncan was going to kiss her. Something she'd dreamed of since high school. Her pulse raced, but she dared not move a muscle and break the moment.

"Daddy! Madison!" Joelle said as she came running into the dining room.

Caleb jerked back as though stung, before turning to face his daughter. "What is it, sweetheart?"

"The movie is done." She looked back and forth between Madison and her dad, a silent question in her eyes.

"Perfect. That means it's bedtime, young lady." Caleb moved around the table, his priorities suddenly shifting gears.

"Aww, but I want to stay with Madison," Joelle whined, proof the little dear was tired.

Caleb shook his head. "Madison was just getting ready to leave. She solved the problem at the store and now our work is done."

"Is that why you were going to kiss her?" Joelle asked, the innocence of her question catching them off guard.

"Yes. A thank you kiss was in order, don't you think?" Caleb asked.

So only one of them was surprised. Caleb, it would seem, had a different agenda than the one Madison played out in her head. It was a lucky escape.

Joelle nodded. "Yup. So, give her one."

Caleb hesitated, drawing in a deep breath. He leaned forward and dropped a kiss on Madison's cheek. A quick, chaste kiss with an *I'm sorry* glint in his eyes.

Not at all like the ones she'd dreamed of in high school.

Talk about a letdown.

Chapter Ten

Last night, Caleb had almost kissed Madison. The feeling leading up to that point had been almost as natural as breathing. It was as though only the two of them existed, a moment in time to celebrate the joy of uncovering the problem at Bigsby's. Joelle's sudden appearance had kept him from making a huge mistake. The problem, however, is that while he knew it was a mistake, it didn't keep him from the disappointment that followed when he stepped away. He couldn't explain it...not by a long shot.

Madison herself had seemed like a deer caught in the headlights, the indecision of her expression enough to make him understand they were both treading on dangerous ground. That he was attracted to Madison scared him. Did it mean he was forgetting Lauren? Is that what people meant about time healing a wound?

He hadn't gone looking for this…a sense of joy at being around someone other than his late wife. And yet it had happened. Hearing the car in the driveway, he knew Madison had arrived, and couldn't help smiling…eager to see her again. And she was right on time, according to his watch.

"Good morning," Madison said when he met her at the door.

"Morning. Joelle's still in bed. I'm guessing it was a late night for her. I didn't want to wake her, but I need to get down to the barn and feed Star, if that's okay with you." It was a good cover for his eagerness to see her and rushing to the door like a schoolboy.

Madison nodded. "Of course. But I was hoping we would have a few minutes to discuss something without Joelle overhearing us."

He was positive the conversation would be the one he had hoped to avoid because honestly, he wasn't sure what to say. This was about the kiss. "Sure thing. Star can wait a few minutes."

"It's just that we didn't talk about it last night, but…" she hesitated, clearly at a loss for the right words.

The least he could do was meet her halfway. "I'm sorry. I shouldn't have tried to kiss you. I was overjoyed at our problem-solving skills, and I got carried away. I hope it doesn't make things awkward between us."

Madison looked away, but not before he saw her jaw tighten. Since when was an apology the wrong thing to say or do?

"No, you don't understand," she said, twisting her hands together. "It's just that we didn't talk about what happens now."

An almost kiss certainly didn't qualify for a serious discussion about the future. "I mean, we're friends…right? Nothing has to happen. I mean, you know my past and I know you're leaving town. It wouldn't make sense to go down this road, would it?" Deep down, he almost wished she would disagree with him…or at least he was confused enough to hope she might.

Madison cocked her head to one side. "What road? Are you talking about almost kissing me?

Because that would have been nothing more than a celebration kiss. No big deal. Right?"

Caleb was more confused than ever. "Then what's this conversation about? What do you want to happen now?"

She shrugged; her brow drawn tight in her careful regard of him. "It's up to you. Do I stay...or do I go? You don't need me anymore as far as I can tell," Madison said.

The light finally clicked. They weren't talking about the same thing...at all. Caleb nodded. "You mean regarding your job here?" He felt like a fool. A bumbling idiot, as though talking to the first girl he ever liked. "Nothing changes. Not yet anyway. Unless you want it to, of course. But Joelle loves having you around and I still need to work at the store. Figuring out what was wrong doesn't mean we can pull the bandage off yet."

Madison's expression changed to one of relief, her smile firmly back in place. "Works for me. I haven't earned enough to pay off the mechanics bill and I want to pick up the car next week. Just in case I get an interview somewhere within driving distance."

He'd foolishly hoped she wanted to keep working for him because she enjoyed it, not because she needed the money. "Well then, consider the nanny job still open and yours. Now I've got to get down to the barn to feed Star if you're sure everything is good between us." A hasty retreat was the best way not to say something he would regret. It's not as though he was looking for a relationship.

Madison nodded. "We're good."

With that settled, Caleb headed to the barn, eager to be alone with his thoughts. Madison had tripped him up on several levels, and he wasn't sure what to do about any of it. The barn door creaked open, reminding him he still needed to fix it.

"Good morning, Star," he said, reaching out to stroke the mare's neck. "Ready for breakfast and to mosey around the pasture a bit while I clean your stall?" he asked, pouring feed into her bucket.

Star nudged him in the arm. Caleb produced an apple and cut it into pieces, offering the treat to the horse. The mare pawed at the ground to show her appreciation. He led her outside, but instead of turning her out, Caleb walked with her, leaving the lead line loose. Not that she needed a lead line. Star had shown him over and over that she would follow Caleb wherever he went. Her trust was all-inclusive.

"So why do you follow me, girl? They say you're one of Sundancer's Legacy horses, but what makes you think I need help?" Star swished her tail at the flies and stomped her hoof.

"My wife died riding a horse, you know. It's why I don't ride anymore. It's nothing personal." Caleb couldn't believe he was talking to a horse, perhaps a reflection of his state of mind and a direct indicator he needed help.

The mare stopped, forcing Caleb to stop and return to her side. "What do you want from me?" he asked.

Star nudged him. "I don't have another apple. Sorry, girl. Life is full of disappointments, you know."

They continued to walk and talk. The horse, of course, never answering. Star went ahead of Caleb, becoming a little friskier. Caleb secured the lead line to keep them at an even pace.

It wasn't long before Caleb spotted Madison and Joelle waving from the backyard. He turned to the horse. "What do you think of Madison?"

Star stopped and nodded her head up and down. "You like her? Well, that makes two of us. I just don't know what to do about it. You know, I never planned on getting involved with anyone again. I planned to focus on Joelle and keep her safe, something I couldn't do for Lauren." The mare whinnied.

"I know, life doesn't come with guarantees. And as much as I like Madison, there's no guarantee with her either. I'm not sure I can handle that gut-wrenching devastation that comes from losing the one you love ever again." Love? It was possible. He certainly never thought it would happen, didn't want it to. But now it seemed entirely possible. The question was, what did he do about it?

Caleb watched as Joelle and Madison played, laughing, and chasing after a ball. His daughter's joy had grown over the past week, and she was a happier child. The question remained, was Caleb happier? And did he deserve to be?

Star stayed close but kept leading him toward Madison and Joelle. Was the horse trying to tell him something? And did he want to listen? Madison's laughter reached his ears about the same time as Joelle's squeals of delight. It was a peaceful sound. The sound of home. And family.

And as to keeping Madison around, it had been an excellent decision. A win/win one that allowed him to work at the store, all while he had a design expert in the mix. Why would he let her go when it would seem he needed her in his home and at work? Madison was good for them both, and it would seem even Star agreed.

Not that the horse ever answered him directly.

Chapter Eleven

♥

"I'm home," Caleb said, dropping a couple of bags on the kitchen counter before he went in search of the others. "Anyone here?" he called out.

Laughter resonated from down the hall. He made his way to Joelle's room, only to find they had outdone the small tent he had made for his daughter. Sheets hung from each corner of the room, draped and decorated with hanging paper ornaments. Comforters and pillows on the ground had been arranged artfully for a tea party with Joelle's dolls. The two of them didn't notice him standing in the doorway. Caleb grinned, unable to hide the surge of feeling in his heart as he watched his daughter. Joyful laughter he hadn't seen much of in the past eighteen months. At least not until Madison showed up in their lives.

"Sounds like too much fun going on."

They looked up at him in surprise.

"Daddy, you're home," Joelle said, running toward him. He kneeled, bracing himself for one giant-sized hug from a pint-sized kid.

"Yes. And I brought us pizza from the shop in town. I figured we should celebrate our good fortune, and that Madison deserved a night of relaxation, not work."

"Yummy, I love pizza," his daughter said, rubbing her belly.

"Hopefully no anchovies or onions," Madison quipped as she stood, straightening her shirt, and running a hand through her hair as if to comb it.

Caleb reached out to help; the action as natural as the air he breathed. She managed to smooth her hair without his assistance and his hand dropped to his side. While he was in town, he'd come to the realization they did need to talk about the kiss last night, and his even odder reaction this morning. The truth was it wasn't a kiss of gratitude he wanted to give her. The idea of spending time with Madison made him happy, and clearly, his daughter felt the same way. *How could it be wrong?* A familiar guilt assuaged him, but he tamped it down this time. It wasn't easy letting go, but perhaps it was time to make way for happiness in their lives.

"No anchovies, but there are onions. Sorry. Guess I should have asked. Can you pick them off?" Caleb asked.

Madison nodded. "Of course. I love cooked onions, but they don't love my breath," she teased.

"Planning on getting close enough to kiss someone?" he asked, unable to resist baiting her. Laughter and teasing were fast becoming addictive...at least with Madison.

"Hardly," she said, her face and throat turning bright pink.

"Then onions it is. Your secret is safe with me." They headed down the hall and Madison set the table as he opened the pizza box and started to serve slices onto each plate. One for Joelle, two for the adults. "And yes, sweetheart, if you want another piece, you can have one," he said, ruffling his daughter's hair as he handed her the plate.

"Does that mean I can have more as well?" Madison asked, her eyes smiling with laughter.

Caleb raised an eyebrow. "Of course. I didn't take you as a three-slice person. You seem to keep surprising me every step of the way."

"Maybe I've worked up an appetite today." She grinned. "Either that, or I'm a glutton for pizza."

Apparently, Madison wasn't one of those girls who counted every calorie going in and out. "Time will tell."

"What do you mean?" she asked.

"Just that next time I see you eating pizza, I'll be counting to see if you're a three-slice regular." Caleb chuckled, taking a bite of his pizza.

"Assuming there *will be* a next time," Madison said, sitting down at the table to join them.

"Oh, I'm positive there will be. This is too much fun, not to repeat. Don't you agree?" It was a huge step forward for Caleb, and it left him slightly off-kilter.

Madison's gaze widened. "I concur, but I wasn't prepared for you to admit it."

"Well, Star and I had a chat today and she sort of made me see what I was missing." Off-kilter and way too eager to spill his guts. It was as though he couldn't shut off his brain or his mouth. *Sort of.*

"The horse talked to you, Daddy?" Joelle asked, tugging at his shirt.

Caleb nodded, not that he wanted to have this conversation with his daughter. Or, at least not in front of Madison. "She did."

"What did she say?" his daughter asked.

"Star said you were a good girl today and that I should reward you both with a special treat. I bought marshmallows, graham crackers, and chocolate to make smores." It wasn't easy to come up with things to do around a campfire with a child involved, but this would hopefully be a winning move.

"I love smores," Madison chimed.

"Goes right along with three slices of pizza," he teased, shooting her a wink. "I thought we could have a campfire under a beautiful starlit night. We can watch for fireflies too." Romance by firelight. It would be an excellent way to test the waters and see if he could even go in this direction. But of all the women he knew, Madison was the only one he felt inclined to test the theory with.

"I love fireflies. Did you know they talk to each other by flashing their yellow lights?" Joelle asked, beaming up at Madison.

She shook her head. "I didn't. But that sounds seriously cool."

"Daddy taught me that. Right, Daddy?"

"Absolutely. Finish eating your pizza and I'll get the fire started outside."

"Yay." Joelle picked up her slice of pizza and ate it, proving that motivation was a great cure-all for slow eaters.

Caleb headed out the back door and grabbed a few logs from the woodpile. He wasn't above using a couple of Fatwood firesticks that were made from old pine stumps that produced an all-natural resin for a quick start.

Within minutes, he had the wood stacked into the shape of a teepee and a flame burning from the center, licking at the logs as it continued to grow. The back door opened, and his daughter came running toward him.

"I'm here. How do I cook a smore?" she asked, stopping all too close to the firepit.

Caleb reached out and put his hand in front of her, just in case. "First, how about backing up some? You need to be calm around a fire as one wrong move and you could get burned and it would really hurt."

"I wouldn't like that, Daddy," Joelle said, shaking her head with exaggerated moves.

"Exactly. So you need to pay attention to the instructions." Madison joined them, holding her hands out to the flames as they licked higher.

"Don't burn yourself, Madison. Daddy says it will hurt really bad."

"I'll be careful. Thanks for the reminder," Madison said, shooting Caleb a grin.

"I found a nice green twig from a long branch on the tree over there," he said, pointing toward the large maple tree nearby. "I've cut off the leaves and sharpened the point. Now you just need to slide the marshmallow on the end and hold it over the fire," he explained, holding up the stick for inspection.

"Did you use your knife?" Joelle asked, reaching out toward the knife.

Caleb nodded. "I did." He took her hand and gently let her touch the point. "This is very sharp and also very dangerous."

"Can I make my own stick with your knife?"

"Like I said, knives can be dangerous. So maybe when you're about fifteen." Caleb laughed, grinning at Madison.

"Do I need to make my own?" Madison asked, just as he handed her the other stick.

"No. I took care of both of you. Just remember, I've made them extra-long, so you don't have to get too close to the fire." Just because he was opening his heart to Madison, didn't mean he would give up his protective ways.

"Then how do I cook it?" Joelle shifted her gaze to the bag of marshmallows and then back at him.

"Hold it over the fire and keep turning the stick until the marshmallow is nice and golden brown. Like this," he said, sliding a marshmallow on the stick and then holding it high above the flames.

"Or you can do it my way and stick it in the fire until it flames up," Madison said, making good on her suggestion. Within seconds, orange and blue flames licked at the soft marshmallow, quickly turning it ashy and black. She blew out the flame.

"You're going to eat that?" Joelle asked.

"I am." Madison slid the gooey mess off the stick and moved to sandwich it in between two graham crackers, neatly tucking a piece of chocolate next to the warm marshmallow.

"That looks yucky," Joelle said, her face scrunched up tight. "I want to do mine your way, Daddy."

Caleb had never understood why people would burn the marshmallow to a crisp, but he figured to each their own. "Agreed. It does look yucky." He chuckled.

It took a while, but the first toasted marshmallow was ready. He took the stick from Joelle, and they headed to the table with the crackers and chocolate. "Watch and learn." He made the gooey sandwich and handed it to Joelle.

"*Mmmm*. I love smores. Yummy in my tummy." Joelle polished it off in record time for a slow eater. She picked up the stick and held it out. "Can I have another one, please?"

"Of course," he said, eager to please.

"Except it's your dad's turn to have one. Perhaps I'll cook his while he helps you," Madison offered, her grin alerting him she was up to no good.

"I've seen the way you cook a marshmallow and it's called burned to a crisp. Thanks, but no thanks." Caleb grinned. "I'll wait until the next round."

"Suit yourself," Madison said, prepping her stick for another flaming treat.

After they finished the special dessert, the adults gathered around the campfire while Joelle ran and chased after the fireflies that were making an appearance as it got dark outside.

Caleb acted on the moment, seeing as they didn't get much time alone. "I've got an admission to make now that Joelle is out of hearing range."

"Oh, what's that?" Madison asked.

He took a deep breath and exhaled, gathering up his courage. "I'm glad you're here. And not just as the nanny. I didn't explain myself very well this morning and I don't want you to leave with the wrong impression. Last night, I almost kissed you because I wanted to, not just out of joy at our discovery. I mean, yes, it was exciting to figure out what was happening, but it's more than that, I fear."

Madison cocked her head to the side. Combined with her questioning gaze, Caleb suddenly felt like an idiot.

She leaned in closer. "You were doing well until the fear part. Last time I checked, fear is a negative, and not exactly a good thing when one is trying to say they like someone," she teased, her award-winning grin firmly etched on her face.

"I'm saying this all wrong, but I'm out of practice. Truthfully, I never expected myself to even consider anything remotely like a relationship with another woman." Caleb held out his hands to the fire to warm them, giving him something else to focus on. He probably shouldn't have said a word, because now everything was out in the open. And complicated.

"I get it. Lauren was a special woman," Madison said, her voice low and filled with compassion.

Caleb gazed at her. "And so are you. We are blessed to have you in our lives. It almost seems as though my heart is thawing, whether or not I deserve it."

"Lauren loved life, and she loved you. It's also the same reason she would want you to move on with life. Be happy. And she would want Joelle to be happy." Madison reached out her hand and he clasped it firmly in his own.

"I'm beginning to believe someone can find another special person in their life, though it's scary. I just want to do the right thing for everyone, especially Joelle. She is my number one concern."

Madison nodded. "I get it. And since you're being honest, I should tell you something as well." It was the barest hint of a whisper, but Caleb heard her.

"Daddy, Daddy...did you see me? There are so many fireflies."

"Looks like fun. But you're also out of breath. Why don't you sit for a while? It's almost bedtime and you've got to unwind if you're ever going to sleep."

Caleb was more than a little curious about what Madison had been about to tell him, and before she left tonight...he was determined to find out. Especially given she hadn't said no.

Almost an hour later, Caleb had Joelle tucked in for the night. Luckily, his daughter had requested Madison's presence for the whole process, which made it easy not to have her leave before they had a chance to talk privately.

Madison picked up her sweater from the sofa. "I've got to head out. Wouldn't want my mother calling you to check on me since I missed dinner."

He didn't want her to leave yet. "I'll walk you to your car," he said, helping her with the sweater, and then followed her outside into the cool evening.

Madison hesitated, and Caleb stepped forward. "You started to say something earlier before Joelle interrupted us. Care to finish that bit of conversation?"

"I kind of hoped you had forgotten." Her nervous laugh left him more intrigued.

"Not likely."

"Well, it's just that after what you said, I figured you should know I had a crush on you in high school." Madison's gaze never left his face.

Her admission was not at all what Caleb expected, but it seemed to have a calming effect on him. "I see. And why didn't you ever say anything?"

"I was going to that night at the dance. Women's lib and all. But then I introduced you to Lauren and the rest...you already know. It was just a crush, so don't worry. I was so happy Lauren had you to love her."

Caleb wasn't sure of much at this moment, but he was sure he wanted to kiss Madison. Could he love again? And was Madison the woman with a key to his heart? "So, you got over the crush, but what about now? Any feelings?"

Madison shrugged, her shy smile tugging at the corners of her mouth. "Maybe."

Caleb leaned forward and kissed her on the mouth. Soft and sweet came to mind. "Me too," he said, stepping back to open her door. They both needed to think about the step they'd taken tonight, having crossed a line that couldn't be undone. Not that he wanted to, but the big picture still loomed heavily in front of them.

For Caleb, it was about letting go of the past, which it would seem he was willing to do. And for Madison, it was about committing to sticking around town. Neither one of them knew what the future held, but for the first time in a long time, Caleb was ready to face the challenges of "what if."

Chapter Twelve

♥

Saturday and Sunday should have been relaxing off days. Instead, Madison had spent most of her time thinking about Caleb. The problem started with the kiss. An innocent kiss, but one that had her reliving the days of her high school crush. It was a dream come true kiss and better than she could have imagined.

Then there was the guilt of kissing a man who had once been married to a friend of hers. But the worst part was admitting to herself that what she was feeling couldn't be labeled a crush. Love in the making...perhaps, or more than a little likely. Spending the past week with Caleb allowed her to see and understand him better. Overly protective but loving. Controlling but sweet and caring. A man capable of deep love, but Madison wasn't so sure he could repeat what appeared to have been a perfect relationship with Lauren.

If she believed him, then Caleb was more than ready to try. But if she believed him and it didn't work out, it was Madison who would be left with a broken heart. And then, there was Joelle to consider and the impact on her. Agonizing over what to do hadn't solved anything.

After settling in to watch Sleepless in Seattle, one of her favorite movies, she pressed play. Perhaps her choice for tonight's movie echoed her hope that Caleb, too, could move forward and fall in love a second time, just like Sam Baldwin. If only to convince herself, the two of them had even the slightest chance of making a go of things together.

As the opening credits played, she checked her phone for messages. No texts, but there was an email. Madison clicked on the icon and then on the email, immediately recognizing the sender. *Sun Glow Fashions* had been one of the companies she had applied to but had given up on since she never heard back.

She scanned the email, a sense of excitement welling within her with each word she read. They wanted her to interview with the company. It was a big step in the right direction, considering it was for a junior designer position, not an office gopher. Or at least she hoped it wasn't a job title masked in sheep's clothing like her last position.

Her excitement hit def-con level ten as she pictured herself sitting at her desk and designing fashions, the results of her hard work showing up in fashion magazines and on the runway, with a model showing off her designs to the most influential people in the business from around the world.

A minute later, the joy subsided to a level three or four. California was a long way away from Dover. It would mean leaving her mother, Caleb, and Joelle. But nothing could change the fact that this was the sort of opportunity she'd worked her entire life for. Not a gopher. Not a nanny.

A fashion designer.

Madison picked up the remote and turned the movie off. Now wasn't the time to encourage her inner self that this could be a lasting love when it wouldn't last past the next couple of weeks if she got the job. It was a big if, but she had to try.

Caleb was a big if also, but she didn't have years invested in the relationship. Of the two, there wasn't much choice. There was no way she could give up a lucrative career opportunity for an "if" with Caleb.

Monday morning, Madison arrived at the ranch house. She'd been dreading the moment she would have to tell Caleb about the job offer. The moment she connected the dots and realized that the company's offer to fly her to California with all expenses paid could only mean one thing...they were serious about hiring her. It was also the moment the dread pitted low in her stomach and continued to grow with each passing hour.

Knock. Knock. Without waiting for an answer, she walked into the house. Early on it was the protocol she and Caleb had arranged.

"Good morning," Caleb said, smiling at her as she entered the dining room.

"Good morning."

"I trust you slept well." His expression held a wealth of meaning as his gaze never left hers.

Madison nodded. She knew exactly what he was asking, but the words she rehearsed were sadly nowhere to be found.

Joelle came skipping into the room. "Hi, Madison. Can we make pancakes for breakfast? You know, the kind with the chocolate happy face and whipped cream?"

Saved from answering Caleb, Madison was ready to promise the little darling the moon. "I don't see why not. Are you hungry?"

"I am. I'm a growing girl. That's what daddy always tells me." Joelle shot her father a look as if seeking confirmation.

"I do say that. But not so fast for breakfast. I was wondering if you two ladies would rather go to the diner this morning to eat. There are a few things I want to check out at the store and wondered if you'd like to tag along," Caleb offered.

"I'd like that, Daddy. They don't do smiley faces like Madison, but they let me color a picture and then they hang my drawing on the wall like I'm a real artist."

"That sounds like fun. I reckon I wouldn't want to get in the way of a budding artist," Madison teased. At least out in public, there wouldn't be any time for private conversations with Caleb.

An hour later, Joelle had eaten her fair share of pancakes and finished her drawings. Her artwork had been hung, and the breakfast bill paid. Together they all walked to Bigsby's, each of them flanking his daughter and holding her hands.

Like a real family.

The overhead bell rang as they entered.

"Hi Tommy," Caleb waved and greeted the kid at the register. "Is my uncle in?"

"Hiya, Mr. Duncan. He left to run an errand but said he wouldn't be gone long," Tommy said, a friendly smile at the ready.

"That's okay. I'm just going to have a look around and see what we can do to move more products. People pay good money for marketing plans, and I figure I've got access to a design consultant," he said, grinning at Madison.

"So, you brought me to work, not play. I see how it is," Madison teased, as Tommy walked away. But deep down, it stung a wee bit. She was a nanny, at least for now. And she wasn't even close to a marketing expert, although she'd offered her services to help analyze his financial records. She could only hope this nanny job didn't become like her last one. *Hire her and then expect more.*

"Only if you want to. And I was referring to the mannequins." Caleb pointed to the clothing section of the store. "They are boring. Not to mention sloppy," he said, lowering his voice a notch with a quick glimpse at where Tommy stood.

"Now that sounds more like something I can do," Madison exclaimed. Perhaps she'd been hasty about lumping Caleb in the same group as her ex-boss. Her esteem rose a notch, knowing in his own way he was admitting she had a level of expertise in the area. Something she wasn't sure that he had taken seriously in the beginning.

"Daddy, can I play with my dolls? Grown-up work is boring."

Caleb nodded. "Sure thing, sweetie. Let me grab a blanket and spread out a play area, and you can have a tea party."

Joelle shook her head. "A birthday party. Madison and I had a tea party yesterday," she said, her tone quite serious.

"I see. Good thinking," Caleb said, shooting Madison a wink.

Madison enjoyed feeling as though they were co-conspirators in the parenting world. She moved off to start work on the mannequins. Soon, the first one was finished, and she found herself in conversation with one of the customers. Interesting woman, Mrs. Jamison. Full of information and a willingness to talk. Small-town gossip at its finest.

Caleb returned and looked up at her handiwork. "I see I've got the right person on the job. Maybe I should hire you...when I can afford another employee, that is." He grinned.

It was the perfect opening, especially with Joelle nowhere in hearing range. "About that, there's something I need to tell you. Last night I received an email from one of the fashion companies I applied to, and I have a job interview."

"That's great news. Congratulations," he said, his broad smile warm and genuine.

"Thanks. I'm excited. They are flying me to their headquarters, all expenses paid. I'm guessing they are serious." There was no way to tamp down her excitement, not that she wanted to. Eventually, Caleb would find out the truth, so it might as well be now.

"Flying? As in, it's a long way away, or flying as in a hop to Houston or Dallas?" Caleb's smile faded. Following his kiss, neither was a suitable answer, but one was way worse than the other.

"Flying as in California."

He nodded. "I see." Caleb might see, but judging by his expression, he didn't want to see. Or didn't like what it meant if she got the job.

It was the same for her, and she needed him to understand. "I'm sorry. We didn't get to talk about it the other night, but believe me, leaving you and Joelle makes me not want to go. Except I can't say no. I've worked years for this and now I might have a genuine opportunity to break into the industry and make a name for myself. I wish things could be different. I enjoy being around you both. And the fact is, I haven't gotten the job yet, so there is that. I just need to try. Whatever happens, God will lead me where I need to go."

Caleb let out a heavy sigh and reached for her hand. "I understand. We should make the most of the time we do have together in case it's cut short. We both love having you around and we want the best for you wherever life takes you."

She was grateful for his calm acceptance, as it would make it easier for her to leave. "Thank you for understanding."

"Not a problem. Maybe if you can finish up the other mannequins, I can tidy up around here. Get a sense of organization and perhaps a better way to layout the store to boost sales. I'm not going anywhere, so I have a store to save." And just like that, Caleb was back to his controlled sense of responsibility.

Madison hated that just as he was moving forward in life, she would leave town. It would be all too easy for him to fall back into his old ways. "And I'm going to keep helping you do just that while I'm still in town." It was the least she could do.

"Maybe you won't get the job and I can keep you here forever," he teased.

His comment caught her off guard. Well played, and one she could take one of two ways. It was better not to go the romantic route. "That's not nice. Steal a girl's dreams before she has a chance at them." Madison laughed.

"Never. I have a feeling you will get whatever you want...you're the most determined woman I've ever met."

"Thanks. I think."

"It was a compliment...don't doubt it." Caleb turned and walked away without so much as a hint he might try to kiss her again, leaving her with a sense of disappointment. Talk about mixed signals on her part. She wanted him to kiss her, and she wanted the job. No fairy tale ending in this story.

Cinderella wouldn't have it all.

Chapter Thirteen

♥

Caleb returned home after running some errands in town and stopping by the store. The fashionably smart mannequins reminded him of his dilemma. Not the store kind. He had truly believed that he might have a chance at another loving relationship, but the center of his affection was determined to leave town. And not even in the same county, or state, for that matter. When he commented yesterday about her not getting the job, it had been a joke...but one that selfishly was born of truth.

He parked the car and headed inside, smiling as he heard voices and laughter coming from down the hall. It sounded as though they were having fun in the tent.

"This is your mother and I when we were eight," Madison said, her words stopping Caleb in his tracks.

"We used to climb on top of the gas pumps at the corner gas station, sipping Mountain Dews and watching the Fourth of July parade. We'd get there hours early for what we thought was the best seat in town when they started throwing out candy from the floats."

"Daddy doesn't let me drink soda and I've never seen a parade except on TV. Will you take me to one Madison?" Joelle asked, hope evident in her request.

They hadn't gone to the town celebrations since Lauren's death. There had been nothing to celebrate as far as he was concerned. But hearing Joelle's request bothered him. It was another example of his shortcomings as a father. Why did everyone keep expecting him to just forget Lauren and move on? The time hadn't been right then, and it would seem it still wasn't.

"You need to see a parade in person. If you would like, I can talk to your father about it."

"Yes, please. Madison...I miss my mommy," Joelle said, his daughter's words slicing Caleb's heart in two.

"It's okay to miss seeing her, but know this, she's in your heart every day. And you have her smile...see. This picture is of when she was around your age. You look just like your mother."

"She's pretty," Joelle said.

"Just like you are."

"Why did God want my mommy in heaven?" Joelle asked, her voice cracking as though she were about to cry.

Caleb needed to put a stop to this conversation, but it was a question he had asked himself a million times and still didn't have an answer.

"Sometimes we never know the answer to that. All we can do is believe it was best for her and know that she's in a lovely place watching over you. I once heard that rain is like the tears from heaven washing over you with love from the special people in your life who are in heaven."

Tears flowed down Joelle's face, and Madison leaned in closer to hug her.

"All the things I love, keep going away," Joelle said, her voice barely a whisper.

"What do you mean?" Madison asked.

"My mommy is in heaven. And I love Star, but my daddy doesn't because of Mommy's accident, and he wants to get rid of her. And I heard you say you were leaving."

"Oh, sweetie. I'm so sorry. I may have to leave if I get the job in California, but it's not like I won't come back to Dover and see you. And as for your daddy, you both lost someone you love very much when your mother died, and you're both hurting inside. Your mother's accident was just that...an accident. Unfortunately, your dad only sees Star as a reminder of a past he wants to forget."

Enough. Madison was psychoanalyzing him to his daughter and should stay out of his personal life. Caleb stepped into the room. "I hired you to be Joelle's nanny, not her counselor. I would think I can handle her questions if she would ask me." Caleb shot his daughter a telling look.

"I'm only trying to help. I brought a photo album over for Joelle to see. I hoped it would help her remember her mother, and that I could share stories to help paint a picture of what a special lady her mother was to everyone who knew and loved her."

"I agree she needs to know more, but I'll tell her…when the time is right."

Joelle cried harder and she climbed into Madison's lap. Caleb was shocked that his daughter had turned to Madison for comfort over him. It was a first and not one that settled well.

Madison hugged Joelle tightly, looking over her shoulder up at him. "I'm sorry. You're right," she said, her expression one of remorse.

"Thank you." Perhaps he shouldn't have been listening and stopped the conversation sooner, but he'd wanted to know more about Madison and what made her tick. There was something about her that drew him to her, but they needed boundaries.

Caleb was already considering the possibility of keeping Star. He just hadn't said anything because he hadn't decided. And as to Madison, perhaps it was a good thing she might leave, otherwise, there was no telling how attached Joelle would get. And when a new job took Madison away from Dover, losing her would only hurt Joelle more. Which is probably the same reason he was conflicted. He cared about Madison, but her leaving was probably for the best.

Too bad he couldn't convince himself to believe it.

Madison had shared the album with Joelle because she thought it would be a good thing for the child. Caleb might not agree with her, but then she didn't agree with him either. It left them at an impasse, with the tiebreaker going to Caleb. *He was Joelle's father.*

His response, however, also pointed to the fact the man was emotionally unavailable. And until he made peace with Lauren's passing, he would never be ready to move forward with life.

The afternoon dragged out, the tension on overload. When it was finally time to leave, Madison was more than ready to pack up her things and go. A quiet night at home was exactly what she needed. Her mother was out for the evening with friends and she had the house all to herself.

Or so she thought. Staring at the walls of the living room but unwilling to replay the conversation a hundred more times, she realized boredom had set in.

Madison retrieved her backpack from the front door and pulled out the photo album she shoved in it. Ledger sheets fluttered to the floor. She must have accidentally picked up the papers with the album.

She started to put them in the pack but hesitated. Why not make good use of her time? She had told Caleb she would work on the problem at the store until she left, and this would be a way of keeping her promise. Maybe even a way to smooth things over between them.

Lying in bed, her back propped up with lots of pillows against the headboard, she made herself comfortable. Spreading out the sheets, she opened her computer and put together another chart. She loved playing with numbers, and with any luck, she'd find another problem account that would go a long way to helping the store become profitable again. Over and over, she drew charts, recorded data, then rearranged the data again.

Hours later, a pattern popped up that had her sitting up on the edge of the bed. She rechecked the numbers she'd written, but nothing changed. This was a big development, but also an ugly one.

The numbers didn't lie. Someone at Bigsby's was doing their fair share of tricky business.

She checked her watch. Three a.m. and far too early to call Caleb. Madison tossed her laptop off to the side and restacked the papers. The morning was only hours away, and she was exhausted. Even though what she'd discovered wouldn't be well received, Madison had to push aside her thoughts and count sheep. Anything to get some sleep.

Madison woke to the sound of a notification ping on her phone. She rubbed her eyes, trying to clear her sleepy vision and focus on the screen. Eight a.m. and she was late.

Caleb: Is everything okay? You're late.

Madison: Sorry. Overslept. Up late working on ledgers. We need to talk about what I found.

Caleb: Sure thing. Can I drop Joelle off at your place? I've got an appointment over in Brambleton at ten to talk to someone about taking Star, but I've got to leave now to make it on time. We can meet back later at the house.

Madison: Sure thing. Sorry. Does that mean you're okay with her riding in the car with me now? (Just double checking)

Caleb: Would seem so. I've seen you drive. Slow is good. LOL. Thanks. See you soon.

Madison: Perfect.

Joelle would be upset to see Star go, but it didn't seem like there was anything she could say or do to change Caleb's mind. The horse had a special connection with him, but he wasn't paying attention. As for his daughter, Joelle could use some extra attention on a day like today, and Madison knew exactly what that should look like. A trip to the lake to play on the beach would certainly add some fun to the little girl's life.

Chapter Fourteen

♥

After a deep discussion with the prospective recipient of Star, and a lot of soul-searching on the way back home, Caleb knew what his decision had to be. Star wasn't going anywhere.

The woman seemed too perfect. And not in a good way. It was as though her tale of woe seemed void of emotion. Caleb's' recent insight into the reality of someone in need had his warning bells going off. The woman's actions didn't match her words. Call it gut instinct...but he was almost positive she was a fraud.

And there were his guilty feelings over finding a new home for Star. Someone had gone to a lot of trouble to give him the horse, and he wasn't being very open to the generous act of kindness. Star was a beautiful mare who had somehow attached herself to him and he was being obtuse in his desire to keep a certain distance. Apple treats hardly made up for his reticence.

Caleb was surprised not to see the black Oldsmobile parked out front. Surely Madison and Joelle would have made it back here by now. An image of them mangled in the car on the side of the road spurred him into action.

"Hello? Anyone home?" he called out. Not that he expected an answer. He grabbed a bottle of water from the fridge and pulled out his phone to call Madison. As he took a swig, he spotted a note taped to the door.

Gone to the lake for a quick swim. Be home soon. (probably before you get here)

The lake. Caleb shook his head to clear away the images of what could happen to his daughter. He hit the speed dial for Madison, needing to put an end to her madness before something happened.

The call went to voicemail. The road that led to the lake would take him twenty-five minutes to get there, as it was a winding road through the countryside. What if it was too late? Panic settled in, the overwhelming sense of doom striking him hard in the gut.

He barely even remembered carrying Lauren back to the house. Or the funeral. Those were days he didn't want to remember...*or repeat*. Caleb grabbed his keys and ran outside to his truck. As he pulled open the door, he spotted Star near the fence, almost as though she were calling him. He paused just long enough to consider his options, but there was only one.

If he rode through his property, cutting straight through to the back side, it would cut off fifteen precious minutes. Caleb slammed the car door shut and ran to the barn, the mare following him in approval.

He grabbed a bridle and slipped it on Star. "Good girl. We can make better time this way. Hope you don't mind bareback seeing as I don't have time to hook up the saddle." Caleb moved to the left side of Star and pulled himself up, sliding one leg over without so much as a second thought. Riding was as natural as breathing, and clearly, he hadn't missed a step. "Giddy up," he said, giving the mare a slight tap with his heels.

Star bolted forward, as eager to make the run as he was...albeit for different reasons. Worry settled foremost in his thoughts, but as time ticked by, Caleb couldn't avoid the inevitable. Riding was in his blood, and this was like coming home. His connection with Star was practically seamless as she followed his gentle signals, as though she understood his urgency. But the fresh air, the sunshine, and the wind on his face couldn't be ignored. Star was a combination of grace and power, and somehow everything around him comforted Caleb.

Joelle would be fine. She just had to be. That Madison had taken his daughter to the lake without his permission, however, was upsetting. The weather was expected to change, and if a storm hit, they would be caught out in it at the lake. Hopefully not in the water. Caleb eyeballed the sky, relieved only a few clouds had moved into the area.

Madison didn't understand his overprotective side, and it was hard to explain in a way she would understand and accept. Perhaps no one could ever take the place of Lauren or love and protect Joelle the way he could. Lucky for everyone involved, Madison had an interview and, for the first time, Caleb realized it was providential. He simply couldn't have a relationship with someone who would jeopardize his daughter and not respect his wishes, even if they seemed extreme. How could he trust her judgment in the future?

Madison had a flighty, irresponsible side he didn't appreciate. Just like when she quit her job and took up dog walking until she found a new one. Not a good, stable decision. And neither was taking Joelle to the lake...especially considering the potential for a storm. Caleb drew up short and gazed over the sea of people on the beach. *Fools...all of them*. Relief filled him when he spotted Madison and Joelle off to the side.

Caleb slid off the horse, and they walked to where Madison and Joelle were having a picnic. He dropped the reins and closed the distance to pick his daughter up, grateful she was okay. "What do you think you're doing here at the lake? You should have asked me first and I would have told you no," he said, directing the question at Madison.

"Daddy, you came," Joelle shouted, smiling as his words and tone went over her head.

"Caleb? What's wrong?" Madison said, coming to stand next to him. Her smile had vanished as worry settled in like a dark cloud over her head.

"You should have never brought Joelle here without my permission. What part of that don't you understand?" Worry had pushed his anger over the edge.

"Daddy, you rode Star. Let me go see her. Will you take me for a ride?" Joelle asked, not in the least bit interested in his conversation with Madison.

"Yes, honey, I rode Star here because Daddy was worried about you, and it was the fastest way to get to the lake." He set Joelle down. "You can go say hi to the Star but keep a safe distance please. I'll be there in a minute, and we can ride back to the house together."

"Yay. I didn't want to leave the lake cause we were having so much fun. But I want to ride Star." Joelle's smile was like a ray of sunshine. Warm and wonderful.

Caleb turned back to Madison. He wasn't the only one unhappy with the current situation, judging by her expression and the firm set of her jaw.

"The part I don't understand is that you hired me as Joelle's nanny, and not once did you tell me I needed permission to do things with her. And you permitted her to ride in the car with me before. What is your problem?"

"Did you know it's about to storm? There's a thirty percent chance of a pop-up thunderstorm in the area. Joelle could catch a cold, or worse, be struck by lightning." He glanced up at the sky, but so far, the weather pattern was holding with only a few white clouds rolling overhead.

"Which means there's a seventy percent chance we won't have one. Yes, I'm aware of the weather and keeping a close watch on it. I prefer to see life from a positive view and adjust when needed. Otherwise, chances of something happening can ruin your fun every time."

"Not good enough. What if you were swimming and lightning struck? They say it can travel ten miles."

"The minute there was any evidence of a storm, we would have left. Look around, Caleb. Lots of people have the same idea and are enjoying the gift of a beautiful day." She stepped back to allow him to see just how many people were still frolicking in the water and playing on the beach.

"They can make their own decisions," Caleb snapped.

"It's important to find happiness and joy in all that you do. You can't stop living and that's what you're trying to do. I think this is more about your overprotective tendencies."

Caleb was stunned by the direct hit of criticism. "What does it matter? Joelle is my daughter. And we won't have to worry about your decision-making moving forward because you're fired." The spur-of-the-moment decision slipped out before he could think it through. He hoped he hadn't just made a colossal mistake, because the sickening feeling that filled him told him otherwise.

Madison stood stock still, her eyes wide and blazing. "You're firing me because I brought her to the lake? Wow. Didn't see this coming. But it certainly makes things easier for me to leave."

Caleb nodded. "I agree. Perhaps this is best for everyone concerned."

She had no intention of letting him know his lack of trust hurt her deeply. But it was better to find out now than later. It would seem Caleb was incapable of change and letting go of the past. Which meant they could never have had a future. "Well, okay then. Nice to see you riding Star, even if the reason wasn't a good catalyst." Madison would do her best to part on better terms, for Joelle's sake.

"I did what I had to do," Caleb said, not backing down.

"I see. Since you promised Joelle a ride back, I'll haul our picnic supplies to the car. Then I'll coordinate dropping off the car when my mother can pick me up," she said, not wanting anything more from the odious man.

"I don't mind giving you a ride home after," he conceded.

Madison shook her head, unwilling to accept anything from him. "That's okay. It's better this way." Tossing his words back at him gave her a sense of satisfaction, even if only for a few seconds.

"Whatever you want." Caleb turned and started walking away.

Madison remembered what she'd discovered about Bigsby's. It was information Caleb needed to know, and she wouldn't leave him in the lurch. After she told him, what he did with the information was all on him. The man was in charge of his destiny and didn't want her help. "One more thing," she said, closing the distance between them.

Caleb stopped and turned, one eyebrow quirked upward in his odd questioning way.

"Last night when I left, I accidentally ended up with a stack of your ledgers with my photo album. And when I found myself restless, I settled in to go over them again to see if there was anything else we might have missed." They both knew why she would have been restless. Her thoughts all centered on Caleb and the kiss, not that any of that mattered at this point.

"Go on," he said, noncommittally.

"Remember when we were at the store the other day?"

Caleb nodded.

"When I was walking around, I never noticed a BOGO display. And then last night, when I was checking over the numbers, a strange but nasty coincidence occurred to me. The decline in profits exactly matches the BOGOP entries. *Every time.*"

Caleb frowned, glancing back at Joelle. He crossed his arms over his chest as he let out a deep breath. "And what do you think your discovery means?"

"I think either your uncle or Tommy is stealing from you. And honestly, I think it's your uncle because he's the only one with access to the books." She hated to be the bearer of such dreadful news, but he had a right to know the truth.

"My uncle isn't stealing from me. He's done his best to step in and help when I needed him the most. And I wouldn't think Tommy is capable either, as he seems to be a good kid. You must be mistaken."

Madison rolled her eyes. "I found the problem, whether or not you like it. Every time the BOGOP account goes higher, the deposit comes up lower, almost dollar for dollar. And don't forget, there was no BOGO display any of the times we were there." She hadn't been paying much attention, but now it was suddenly relevant.

"You're forgetting I told my uncle to stop the BOGOs, so perhaps he took down the display and sent the items back for a credit to help the store. So, you see, there's a perfectly good explanation. And not one that implicates my uncle."

"But your explanation doesn't explain the number matches. Do what you want with the information, but I'm telling you to look deeper." Madison shrugged, ready to wash her hands of the entire matter.

"Thanks for the information and your help in figuring out what was going on. I'll investigate the matter, not that I feel my uncle is complicit."

"Well, all right then. I should pack up and be on my way. At least I'll have more time to prepare for the job interview. I'll let you know when I'm coming over to drop everything off."

"Sounds good." Caleb turned and headed to where his daughter and Star waited.

Madison followed and hugged Joelle. "Maybe I'll see you at the house later." A chance to say goodbye. Otherwise, Caleb would have the honor of explaining why he fired the nanny.

"Okay. I'm going to ride on Star. I'm so excited," Joelle said, her eyes glowing. "Bye, Madison."

She would miss Joelle with all her heart. And Caleb too. But sometimes life didn't turn out the way you wanted it to.

And sometimes it did.

All she had to do was get the job.

Chapter Fifteen

♥

Joelle hadn't been understanding in the matter of Madison when Caleb explained why she wouldn't be her nanny any longer. His daughter had worn a frown like a grumpy girl who didn't believe the sun would ever shine again. The two had tearfully hugged goodbye when Madison dropped the car off. He appreciated Madison's efforts to make things right between him and Joelle, impressing upon his daughter it was only a matter of days before she would have had to leave anyway for the interview.

As of this morning, Joelle was finally talking to him again. Dealing with a daughter who thought he had dropped the moon into permanent darkness by cutting Madison out of their lives made the days drag on.

Caleb parked the truck, all the while going over in his head what to say to his uncle. Asking questions without revealing the "why" he was asking wasn't an art he had ever learned, much preferring straightforward, to-the-point conversation. Except this was his uncle.

Madison had to have this all wrong, and it was simply a coincidence. Or Tommy was craftier than they gave him credit for. "Did you bring your dolls?" Caleb asked.

Joelle nodded. "Yup."

"Good. I need you to play a bit while I talk to Uncle Bill about some things."

"Okey dokey. After, can we go to the beach? It's a sunny day. I want to play in the water, and I didn't get to the other day. And then can we go for another ride on Star? I want to have fun."

"We'll see." It was the best answer Caleb could give. It's not that he was against fun, only the dangers that seemed to go hand in hand with adventure. But riding Star...had him thinking of the past. The good parts, that is. And he missed them.

The overhead bell jingled as they entered the store. "Good morning, Mr. Duncan. What brings you here today?" Tommy smiled, greeting him as though nothing was amiss.

"Good morning. Is my uncle in the back? I need to speak to him." He preferred to get this over with and not deal with small talk.

Tommy shook his head. "No. He had to leave in a hurry but said he wouldn't be gone long."

His uncle seemed to be out of the store more often than Caleb appreciated. How could Bill manage the place properly if he was never there? "I reckon Joelle and I will wait in the office and stay out of your way."

"Gotcha."

"Oh, and Tommy, quick question. What happened to the BOGO display?"

Tommy frowned. "This may sound terrible considering I work here and all, but I don't know what you're talking about. I've never heard of a BOGO. What is it?"

Caleb took a deep breath. Strike two against his uncle. Something was seriously wrong, but there had to be some other explanation. His uncle wouldn't steal from him or his great-niece. "It's a promotional thing and stands for buy one, get one free. Do you have anything like that in the store?"

The kid shook his head. "No. I'm here every day and that's nothing we've done in all the years I've worked here. Why?"

Caleb swallowed hard, unable to wrap his head around the information. "Okay, thanks. I was just curious, but don't worry about it. Come on, Joelle, you can play in the office this time since Uncle Bill isn't here."

"Can I swing around in his chair?" She grinned.

"Of course." He led her to the office and after a few spins, she settled onto the floor, content to play with her dolls. Which left Caleb time to think...and stew. He didn't want Madison to be right because the truth would be an ugly reality. He clung to the belief there had to be another explanation, but he was no longer shutting out the possibility.

Joelle crawled under the desk, using it as a house. "Daddy," she said, crawling out from the darkened space, "I found a paper. Here." His daughter placed what appeared to be a small receipt in his hand.

"Thanks, honey. You're a good finder and I'm sure Uncle Bill will appreciate this." Joelle crawled back into her play space, as Caleb inspected the paper he held. Much to his surprise, it was a horse race ticket stub for next week's Texas Classic race.

Caleb frowned. Was his uncle betting on horses? It wasn't anything he ever remembered his uncle talking about, and the owner of this ticket was doing some serious betting. This bet was to the tune of two grand. Madison's words from yesterday came back to mind. Sizeable sums to BOGOP, and lower deposits from sales that matched. And according to Tommy, there had never been a BOGO display.

Maybe the ticket belonged to someone else. It's not like there was a name on it or anything. He spotted the trashcan next to the desk. Left with no choice, Caleb rifled through the trash. Toward the bottom, he found two more of the blue tickets wadded up in a ball. He uncurled each one, and the truth hit hard. His uncle had a gambling problem, and it would seem he was using Bigsby's to foot the bill.

Caleb's gut clenched, the betrayal making him sick to his stomach. At least until rage settled in its place. He pocketed the tickets and then searched the desk but didn't find anything else. Not that he needed more proof to add fuel to the fire. Pacing the room, he waited for his uncle, determined to have it out with him.

The man deserved to be in jail, not running his store. All this time, Caleb had believed in his earnest offer to help after Lauren died. Discovering the offer was motivated by greed appalled him. For his mother's sake, he wouldn't turn his uncle over to the police, at least he wouldn't if his uncle agreed to his terms. Bill was still family, and Caleb had to help him.

"Hey, how's my favorite little girl?" Uncle Bill said from the doorway, a smile at the ready.

Joelle scooted out from under the desk and ran toward him. Part of Caleb didn't want his daughter to even have contact with someone capable of such deceit, but he wouldn't involve Joelle in the situation's ugliness. "We've been waiting for you. And guess what? I found a paper you lost. Daddy said I was a good finder."

"Why thank you," Uncle Bill said, the lines on his forehead deepening as he turned his focus back to Caleb.

"Joelle, why don't you take a couple of dolls and play behind the register for a minute?"

"Sure thing, Daddy." Joelle grabbed one doll and headed to the sales floor. Caleb followed, stopping at the doorway. "Hey Tommy, can you keep an eye on Joelle for a bit?"

"Sure thing, Mr. Duncan. Come on pip squeak," Tommy said, holding out his hand. With Joelle settled, Caleb closed the door and turned to face his uncle, who had moved to sit at the desk.

"What brings you here?" Uncle Bill asked, looking more out of sorts with each passing second.

Caleb tamped down the anger threatening to spill over. It wouldn't do any good and how he handled this could affect the outcome. His uncle's decision would need to be his own. "As you know, the store has been losing money."

Uncle Bill's face grew pale. "I'm so sorry. I did what you asked and stopped the BOGOP orders, but there's little else I can do to turn things around."

"That's not true. I believed in you and trusted you. But these tickets," Caleb said, pulling them out of his pocket and tossing them on the desk, "they tell a different story."

His uncle's face turned ashen. "It's not what you th..th..think."

"Sure, it is. You might as well tell me the truth because I'm not leaving until I understand why you would do this to us. Stealing is wrong at all levels, but this...you're stealing from family." Caleb shook his head, at a loss for words to explain the devastating impact of his uncle's actions.

Uncle Bill stood, holding the desk for support. "I didn't...you've got this all wrong."

There was no way his uncle could talk his way out of this. "The numbers match. Those tickets, the dates, the BOGO sales that incidentally are non-existent. An elaborate accounting nightmare designed to cover your gambling habits."

His uncle looked on the verge of a breakdown, as though his entire life was flashing before his eyes. "I..."

"The truth," Caleb said, taking a step forward.

"I'm sorry. I didn't plan this when I took over the store. Please believe me." Suddenly, his uncle looked old. As though he'd aged ten years right before Caleb's eyes. He dropped back into the chair and slumped forward on the desk, refusing to look at Caleb.

"Then what happened?" Caleb asked, not willing to stop pressing for answers until he knew the whole story. His uncle's addiction would have cost him the store and possibly the house if it hadn't been for Madison's discovery.

"It started with just small bets. But then the excitement...and the need to recover what I was losing got to me. I was stuck and had no way out other than to borrow money from a bookie and then I had to keep repaying him. All I ever needed was one big win and I swore I'd quit. I'm so sorry. What are you going to do to me? I know what I deserve, but I beg you, please don't send me to jail. I don't want to live the rest of my life behind bars."

Caleb let out a deep breath. The store would recover under his management, especially given he wouldn't have to pay for a store manager. He didn't want anger at life to continue to control his every decision. "This whole situation is heartbreaking, and you can consider yourself fired...immediately. As for what I'm going to do, I've thought of a plan, but only you can decide your fate."

"A choice is more than I gave you...and I understand you must fire me. What's your deal?" Uncle Bill looked up at him, a glimmer of hope in his eyes.

"You attend gambler's anonymous to deal with the addiction," Caleb said, the option coming to him from out of nowhere. Or more likely, direction from God.

"And the other choice?" Defeat etched every line on his uncle's face.

"Prison. The decision is yours to make."

"GA is good. It's more than I deserve. And Caleb, I promise to pay you every cent back. I can sell the house. Downsize. Anything to make this right."

"Just get help first. Then we can talk about the rest when the time is right. Hand over the keys and bring me proof that you've enrolled within forty-eight hours. And Uncle Bill...no more. Oh, and give me the ticket. Ill-gotten gains wouldn't suffice at a time like this."

"But what if my ticket wins?" Uncle Bill stood, glancing down at the ticket in his hand, his fingers tightly clenching the paper.

"It's not your ticket, so it doesn't matter. It was bought with my money."

Uncle Bill let out a deep breath. The hesitancy with which he handed over the ticket, even now, told Caleb all he needed to know. This would be a tough up-road battle for his uncle. Perhaps one day, they could put all this behind them.

His uncle handed him the store keys and walked out of the office; his head hung low. Caleb had been more than fair with the man, and he only hoped his faith that his uncle would follow through with the plan wasn't misplaced.

Madison had been right all along, and perhaps he shouldn't have been so harsh on her at the lake. Joelle was safe, and it's not like he didn't know she was right about him being overprotective. But letting go didn't come easy.

Just like letting Madison go wasn't easy because, like it or not, he had fallen in love with her. Something he didn't quite understand until he had cut her out of his life.

His feelings for Madison weren't the only thing he was figuring out. There was Star. Riding was a part of who he was, and he'd missed the freedom that came with it. He would ride again, and not just because Joelle would continue to pester him until he took her for another ride, but because he loved it. Even the worry over Joelle hadn't been able to squash the joy. And more than that, he knew deep down he trusted Madison to keep his daughter safe.

He had been running from the very thing he needed to remain constant.

Riding horses.

And he let go of someone he loved and trusted out of fear. It was a deep-seated need to protect his heart.

Madison.

Chapter Sixteen

♥

Madison's mother stood in the doorway that led to the kitchen, a worried expression on her face. "What's the matter, dear? I thought you were supposed to be watching Joelle this morning."

Turning back to the coffeepot, Madison was intent on pouring some of the freshly brewed, much-needed coffee. Last week her mother accepted her request to be picked up at Caleb's after dropping off Lauren's car without the necessity of any explanation. After picking up her car from the garage, Madison managed to spend most of her time in town, hoping to evade her mother's questions about the situation. Now, facing the truth was inevitable. "You might as well know the truth. Caleb fired me."

"Fired you? Why on earth would he do that after all you've done for him and his daughter?" Her mother's tone had grown defensive, always ready to stand up for Madison.

The worst part was…Madison still didn't feel like she had done anything wrong. "Because I took her to the lake, and he didn't approve."."

"I don't understand. What's wrong with that? Please tell me she didn't get hurt." The lines on her mother's brow deepened with worry.

"Nope. Not even close. We didn't even get to swim. But Caleb came riding in on Star, acting like Sir Galahad to rescue Joelle from the silly nanny who dared to let her have fun and live a more normal childhood. Imagine the horror of taking a child to the beach." Each word dripped with disdain, but she was beyond trying to make a good showing for the situation. Caleb had gone over the top, leaving her to look like an incompetent nanny.

"*Hmmm*." Her mother nodded. "It is extreme and surely other people will feel the same. Don't let it bother you, dear. The poor man has been through so much losing his wife, and now you'll never guess what I heard this morning at the grocery store. Not that I believe all the gossip in town, but everyone is saying he fired his uncle Saturday afternoon. Can you imagine?"

Madison snapped to attention. This was news she hadn't heard. "More than likely it's true. I discovered some things about his uncle that I'm not at liberty to discuss, but I relayed them to Caleb. It would seem my information was spot on, not that it's a good thing, mind you." All her anger and frustration with Caleb vanished in a split second. Instead, knowing what it meant, her heart went out to him.

Her mother studied her for a moment, her gaze unwavering, before she moved to the sink to put away some dishes. "They also say Caleb is running the store this morning, and that Joelle is with him, which makes sense now he no longer has a nanny."

Madison was more than a little tempted to drop in at the store, just to see how Caleb was doing. "The town is full of information. Anyway, I agree that Caleb has been through a lot. I mean, I was leaving town eventually, so it's probably for the best I don't get too attached to Joelle. She is the sweetest child ever." *Or Caleb.* But that wasn't something she'd be sharing with her mother, because she cared about him a lot more than she should.

"Sounds to me like you are already attached...to both father and daughter."

"It's not like that. We're just two friends who worked together to figure out some things." In her heart, she knew it was a lie, but it was best to keep the information to herself.

"If you say so. Are you still going to the interview?" her mother asked.

Madison nodded. "I am."

"Pity. California is a long way away. You and Caleb would make a handsome couple and little Joelle is precious. You could find something closer to home, and maybe have a career *and* a family. I've enjoyed having you home, and it's been lonely what with your father gone and then you left town." Her mother folded the hand towel and hung it on the sink door.

They'd been over this before, but this time her mother was ramping up the guilt. "Like I said, Caleb and I are friends. And I'm sorry, but to make one's mark in the fashion industry, it's all about exposure. Something you get from a big city clientele. I'll try to visit more often, but we should enjoy what's left of the time I am here. We could do something fun today." Anything to get her mind off Caleb and Joelle.

Her mother removed the apron she always wore...one of three Madison had picked out for her years ago for Christmas, though *Kiss the Cook* was Madison's favorite. "I'd like that. Maybe we could go to lunch and do some shopping over in Austin," her mother suggested.

"Good idea. I could buy some new shoes to go with the outfit I designed for the interview. I can't wait to show it to you." Madison had spent hours creating the pattern and even more hours sewing the dress, but it was simply perfect, and she was excited to show it off.

"That sounds wonderful. But then all your designs are. Let's meet up in one hour and head out. That will give me some time to finish up a few things."

"Sounds good." Madison made her way to the living room, her gaze drawn to a couple walking hand in hand down the sidewalk. That's what she wanted in her life, a loving relationship. Once again, life was throwing her a curve ball that put a kink in the plan. The job was on the horizon, but the man was here in Dover.

But then love took two people, and Caleb was emotionally unavailable. For a short time, it had seemed he was willing to move forward, but then he'd retreated, putting up a wall between them. It wasn't like she expected them to move to the city, so it was all for the best. She just wished it wasn't so confusing. Caleb wasn't looking for love, which was more proof her mother was wrong.

Madison knew it was the right thing for her to take the interview and give it her best shot. *Onward and upward.*

Every day the routine was the same for Caleb. Get Joelle up, feed her breakfast, and get her dressed, packed, and ready to spend the day at the store. His daughter was growing bored and acting out, not that he blamed her. There were only so many ways Joelle could play at the store, but it's not like he had a choice.

Yet.

If he hadn't fired Madison, she'd still be watching his daughter and Joelle would have fun. He was tempted to call her and apologize, hoping she could help until she found out about the job. Except someone in the store mentioned she was flying out on Wednesday. It wasn't enough time to change the result. He still needed to find someone to watch his daughter.

And as much as he wanted to believe he needed Madison for Joelle; he was honest enough to admit to himself how much he missed her. And it was after he'd tucked Joelle in bed and he was alone, that the void in his heart hurt the most.

Tonight, he didn't want to dwell on all that he'd lost, and he didn't want to think about the store or his uncle. What he needed was Madison's cheerful attitude, but he would have to settle for a movie.

Except when the movie started, he was only vaguely aware of what was happening on the screen. Madison had been right about so many things. What he wouldn't give to undo the words he had said to her, especially given she was right. It was time he faced his fear that danger lurked in every corner, and time he sought professional help to make it work. Lauren's death was an accident.

Letting the accident control his life wasn't good for him or his daughter. It was time to move on, and unfortunately, because of his big mouth, it would be without Madison.

Of course, the new company would want Madison. She was talented, smart, and genuine to the core. They'd be fools not to hire her, just like he'd been a fool to fire her.

"Madison. Madison," Joelle called out, her voice capturing his attention.

Caleb bolted down the hall to his daughter's room. She was tossing and turning on the bed but was still asleep. "Madison. Madison," she cried out again.

He moved to the bedside and cradled his daughter, not wanting to scare her. "Sweetheart, it's daddy. Wake up. You're having a bad dream." He smoothed back her hair off her face as her eyes fluttered open.

"Daddy?"

"It's okay, sweetheart. I'm right here." His heart ached for Joelle, as her eyes shimmered with tears.

"I want Madison. I miss her, Daddy."

Caleb missed her, too. "I know you do. She's going to a job interview. Grownups need to work and, unfortunately, what she loves to do requires her to live in the city."

"It's not fair. Mommy's gone and now Madison's gone too," she cried, hiccupping on a sob.

Caleb cupped the side of her face gently. "You've got me. I can hug you whenever you need someone to lean on, and I'm a good listener."

"I don't want to lean on you. That would make it hard to walk. I want to make cookies. And swim, and ride bikes, and horses. I want to be like other kids, Daddy."

Her words hit him straight in the heart like a lightning bolt. If he didn't wake up and figure out how to live again, he'd lose his daughter. And that would destroy him. "I understand. I'm sorry if I've been going overboard trying to keep you safe. Life is for living, something Madison and Star have taught me. You'll get to do all those things, and you'll make friends at school this fall."

"Promise?" she asked, her voice barely above a whisper.

"Pinky promise," Caleb said, holding up his little finger.

Joelle did the same, and they shook pinkies, his daughter's answering smile a welcome relief. The bond Joelle had made with Madison was proof his daughter could love again. It would seem the real problem lay within him. Trusting in life and love. Again. That was what he needed to move forward. For Joelle's sake, he would do all those things he'd just promised...and he would do them with his daughter.

"Go back to sleep, sweetheart," he said, kissing Joelle on the forehead and tucking the blankets all around her.

"Night, Daddy. I love you."

"I love you, too."

Caleb left the door open a little further this time, just in case his daughter had another bad dream. He had a lot to think about, but first, he needed to call Tommy. The two of them had a long talk after his Uncle Bill left the store, and it was then Caleb learned just how much responsibility Tommy could handle. And needed. The kid had been taking care of his family after his father left. The stress of it all had poor Tommy in a chokehold, his fear of doing something wrong and getting fired in overload. Far from it, it was time Tommy had a promotion and started running the store whenever duty called Caleb home.

Like tomorrow. It was time to honor his first promise to Joelle and take her for a ride on Star.

And if Madison didn't get the job, he'd be right here, waiting to try and win her heart again. He'd been blessed with the love of two magnificent women, and he'd be a fool to let Madison go if there was any chance they could make a relationship work.

Chapter Seventeen

♥

Madison's nerves were on edge, her stomach tight with trepidation. Today was the day of her interview. The sun shone brightly, but it certainly wasn't a reflection of her mixed feelings about what the day would bring. The flight to California wouldn't take long, and her interview was set for four o'clock. It would be a long day, but with any luck, she'd be back in Dover before the end of the day. And if things went as well as she expected, her time back home was nearing an end.

By working as a junior designer, she could afford more necessities, such as a better car. With over two hundred thousand miles, it was time to let Old Nellie go. The thought of leaving Dover was like hitting the repeat button on her life. When she was eighteen, her reasons for moving away had been different. Although perhaps not so different or so it would seem. Both times she went looking for a job to make her happy, and both times Caleb seemed to be in the picture...or more to the point...in it, but not with her.

Her mother stood at her bedroom door. "All packed and ready to go?"

Madison nodded, zipping her small carry-on bag closed. "I am. Just nervous about what the day will bring and contemplating what the change will mean."

"You'll be fine, dear. It would be nice to keep you here, but I understand your need to do this, and I'm behind you one hundred percent. And I love the dress you're wearing. Talk about chic...and it's your design." Her mother ran a hand down the sleeve of the emerald silky fabric, holding up the extra folds of light chiffon to look it over. "They won't want to miss out on your talent. And to think you designed that right here at our kitchen table."

"Thanks, Mom. You've always been my number one fan."

"Honey, you earned my approval. It didn't just come because you're my daughter." Her mother hugged her.

"I guess we'll find out soon enough." Madison picked up her travel bag and made her way down the hall and out of the house. With her head held high, she slid into her car, ready for the challenge. This was something she deserved after years of hard work and dedication.

Old Nellie started right up, and Madison shifted into reverse to back out of the driveway. She turned on some country music and was soon tapping out the beat on the steering wheel. If she didn't think about what she would leave behind, there was less chance she would get tripped up by her emotions. *Focus on the endgame.*

Madison flipped on her blinker and turned onto the entrance ramp to the interstate. After doing a head check for traffic, she accelerated to get up to speed and merge onto the highway. Nellie sputtered and surged forward, but then sputtered again. She checked her fuel level. All good. No engine lights. Nothing wrong that she could tell. *Not again.* "Not now, old girl. We've got places to go. People to meet." Madison tried to speed up again, but this time the car shut off, much like before. "You've got to be kidding me?" What was the point in paying to have the car fixed if it didn't get fixed?

A car blew past and blasted its horn.

"It's not like I chose to stall out in the right lane, mister," she said, her frustration mounting. Madison flipped on the flashers as she tried to figure out what to do. There was no way she could push the car off the road. And unlike last time, she wasn't sitting at an intersection close to home.

She tried to start the car one more time, hoping whatever was wrong would clear itself up. Nothing. Madison tried to remember the rules about situations like this. After checking for traffic, she exited the car, raised the hood, and moved to the side of the road for safety.

Pulling up the map on her phone, she searched for the towing companies near her. She called the one closest to her location, which turned out to be the small town of Norwich. After a short discussion with the mechanic, she was relieved they had agreed to transport Nellie back to Dover. It would cost extra, but the alternative was just as problematic.

The only problem was that they required her to be there to sign for the release, and she was on a tight schedule to get to the airport. The guy promised her he would be there within fifteen minutes and it would still work if she called for a shared ride driver to pick her up. Barely.

Madison sat down in the grass to wait. A few people slowed or stopped to ask if she needed help, but eventually continued their way once she let them know everything was under control. Fifteen minutes came and went. And by the time fifteen minutes had turned into thirty, Madison was worried. She would never make the flight at this rate, considering she still needed a ride to the airport.

Suddenly she felt an odd wet sensation beneath her. Jumping to her feet, Madison realized the ground was still damp from the recent rain and now it had soaked through her designer dress. She twisted the material around to the front and checked the damage. A dirty wet stain added insult to the problem she was already dealing with. "Why me, Lord?" Madison asked, with a shake of her head.

Decision made, Madison fired off an email to the human resources manager at Sun Glow Fashions, letting them know she would miss her flight and was forced to cancel the interview. She fully expected they would move on and find someone else, but it couldn't be helped. At least this way if they wanted to reschedule...they could.

Chapter Eighteen

♥

Caleb looked up from the register when the overhead bell jingled, and a customer walked in. He moved to greet the older woman since Tommy was on a lunch break. "Good morning, Mrs. Stanton. Nice to see you again."

The older woman shook her head. "Normally you wouldn't see me on back-to-back days, but I forgot the wax I needed for my project. There's always something I'm forgetting, or so it seems." The tone of her voice conveyed a deep concern for the issue, but as people got older, it happened far more than they liked.

He smiled, trying to lighten her bad mood. "That just means I get to see you more. At least you don't live far from here."

"True. It's easier for you young folks to *roll with the punches*, or is it *go with the flow*?" Delores frowned.

"I think they mean the same thing. But I'm not sure you can count me in the young folk category." Caleb shot her a wink and was rewarded with a smile.

"Of course you are. Younger than me. Make the best of what God gives you, that's all I'm saying. Just like Cindy Bradley's daughter, Madison. Now that's a real case of going with the flow. She was gone for years up in New York City, lands back in town, and then is ready to take off again. Now that's all changed, poor dear. She had her heart set on that job in California. Nothing I would want, all that travel everywhere. Me, I just want to stay at home and in Dover where I know most everyone."

The minute Delores mentioned Madison, she had his full attention. Understanding what she was saying was an entirely different matter. "What do you mean, changed? Didn't she leave this morning?"

Delores shook her head. "I heard at the coffee shop that her car broke down on the interstate and the tow truck out of Norwich took over an hour to arrive. She should have called Devon Turner. He may be busy being the only garage in Dover, but he wouldn't have left Madison on the side of the road for as long as that other guy did. Not safe for a woman alone like that."

This wasn't the first time Madison had car trouble and he was pretty sure someone at Turner's had done the repairs. Hopefully, it was a different issue...and it was an old car. "So I'm guessing she missed her flight?"

"That's what I'm trying to tell you. Now, where was I? Oh yes, I need paraffin wax. These old hands of mine don't look so good nowadays. Need to soften my skin for a more youthful look, you know, just in case Ed Dugard over in Green-flower wants to ask me out to lunch after church come Sunday."

Caleb had to put an end to the conversation. "Let me get you the wax," he said, moving to the aisle to grab a few boxes since he forgot to ask her how many she wanted. And he need-ed to move her along so that he could close the store. He'd been trying to think of what to say or do when Madison returned from her trip, but it would seem he had the opportunity now. And he wouldn't let the chance to set things straight with her wait another minute.

This was his chance to prove to Madison he had changed his way of thinking and his outlook on life. Her messages had been loud and clear and now it was his turn to show he'd listened. Caleb never closed the store except on major holidays, so this was proof of how important she had become to him.

"Did you want one or two boxes?" he asked, ready to ring up her order.

"Just one. My hands aren't that big." Delores laughed and handed him her credit card.

"You wouldn't know where Madison is now, do you? Is she still at the garage in Norwich, or did she get a ride home?" Caleb wasn't above using the gossip chain to his advantage if it meant getting to Madison quicker.

"Last I heard, she was home." Delores checked her watch. "But I left the diner over an hour ago."

Caleb handed her back the credit card and pushed the package across the counter. "Thanks, Mrs. Stanton. Have a wonderful rest of your day."

Except Delores didn't move, her gaze never leaving his face. "I will. You seem keen on finding out about Madison. You like her or something?" The older woman grinned, her crooked teeth exposed.

Or something. A better word was love, but he wouldn't be sharing that information with Delores. "Just making sure she's all right. She helped with Joelle, and I feel I should help her in return." It sounded plausible.

"Where is the little darling? She's always with you. Best I can recollect anyway," she added, glancing around the store.

"I let her go to a friend's house today instead of coming here."

"Good idea. The girl needs friends. Bye now," Delores said, picking up her package and leaving.

Caleb followed her to the door and flipped the *open* sign to *closed*. People might get upset, but this was too important not to handle this very instant. He locked up and then drove to Mrs. Bradley's house, hoping Madison would still be there. He knew in his heart Madison was special, and he didn't want to let her go. But he also understood he needed to give her the wings to fly. She deserved the future she wanted...had dreamed of. And if it meant she would leave Dover, then he should help her chase those dreams.

It was the very reason he knew he loved her. Loved her enough to put her happiness ahead of him and let her go. With a quick call to a friend of his, Caleb secured transportation for Madison to California...via a private plane. If they hurried, she would still make the interview.

He pulled into the driveway and made his way up the steps.

Knock. Knock.

Madison opened the door, much to his surprise.

"Caleb? What are you doing here?" she asked, glancing around as though looking for Joelle.

"I heard you had car trouble and I'm here to help in any way I can."

Madison looked somewhat confused; her brow furrowed. "My car is a piece of junk and I should quit throwing money down the drain. Where's Joelle?"

"At a friend's house," Caleb said, hoping she would understand the importance of that little tidbit of information.

Madison did a double take. "I thought..."

"You thought right, until recently." He stepped forward and took her hand, drawing her closer. "I should have listened to you sooner, but just know this…I'm making some changes in my life." Her answering weak smile wasn't exactly what Caleb had hoped for. Maybe he'd been wrong about how she felt toward him.

"It's sweet of you to come here, but it's too late. I canceled the interview," Madison said, surprising him with this turn of events.

Caleb shook his head. "Then un-cancel the cancel. You need to get to L.A. and your interview. You've dreamed of this and it's too big of an opportunity to let it slide." He would support her no matter what, the same way she had done for him.

"Thanks, but honestly, it's too late. My flight has already left and there's not another one going out until later tonight. That's why I canceled the appointment. I guess it wasn't meant to be. I figured you would be happy with the change in plans."

He deserved the comment, considering all that he'd said to her before. "That's where you're wrong. I've got a friend who's agreed to fly you to L.A. on a private plane. Just say yes, and I'll drive you to the airstrip in Greenflower. What time's your interview?"

"Four. I can't believe you set all this up." Madison took a deep breath and exhaled, her gaze watching him closely.

"Believe it." He quickly checked his watch. "You have just enough time if we leave now. What do you say?"

"I guess the only thing I can say is yes. It is my dream job."

Except Madison didn't seem all that excited. But then, it wasn't as if he wore his emotions on his sleeve either. "Great. Let me notify Charlie we're on our way." Caleb sent a text to his friend knowing it would take him time to get flight clearance. Luckily, it was a small local airport, which made everything a lot easier.

"Ready?" he asked when she returned to the porch.

"As ready as I'll ever be. And thanks," Madison said, reaching up to kiss him on the cheek.

Caleb's heart swelled ten times bigger with the simple gesture. They headed for the truck, and he held the door open for her. Coming around the back of the vehicle, he slid into the driver's side, started the truck, and backed out of the driveway.

As they headed for Greenflower, Caleb noticed Madison was deep in thought.

She turned to him. "I heard about your uncle. I'm truly sorry. I didn't want to be right about him," Madison said, diving right into the conversation where they left things off.

Caleb nodded. "I know. I should have listened to you sooner, but Uncle Bill is family. I just couldn't believe he would do something so deceitful. But he is getting help, so I'm relieved." They'd only spoken twice, but one day, he hoped they could repair the relationship.

"Most people would have had him thrown in jail," Madison said.

"I like to think I'm not like most people. Would you have turned him in?" He didn't want this between them if she disagreed with his decision. Better to air the issue out in the open.

Madison smiled. "Nope. I loved your compromise. Trust me, the whole town knows. Bill is grateful, and he's singing praises about his nephew to anyone who will listen."

Of course, they were on the same page...he should have known she would understand. "I just think family is important. I can replace the money eventually and we'll be fine. But I have to live with my decision, and I know in my heart it was the right thing to do. Sometimes people make mistakes, and since it only involved me, I figured it was my choice how to handle the resolution."

Madison reached out and touched his arm. "You did good."

"Thank you," he said, turning into the airport and making his way to the hangar where his friend's plane was parked. They got out of the car, meeting at the front end.

"Guess this is it," she said, noticing the pilot headed their way.

"Looks that way. Just one other thing before you go..."

"What's that?" she asked.

Caleb stepped in closer and lowered his head to kiss her. Not a friend's kiss. A kiss to let Madison know the true depth of his feelings, leaving no doubt in her mind.

"Hey, you two. Are we making this flight to L. A. or are you going to stand here and make out?" Charlie asked, laughing at his joke.

Caleb stepped back and grinned, shaking hands with his friend.

"This is Madison, and yes, she's making the flight. Madison, meet Charlie."

"Nice to meet you, young lady. Let's go, shall we?" he said, glancing at his watch. "We only have about ten minutes before my window to get airborne closes."

"Good luck at the interview, Madison," Caleb said, knowing the time had come to let her go.

"Thank you for everything," she said, waving as she and Charlie boarded the plane.

No matter what happened in the future, Caleb would never regret kissing Madison. His heart was beating faster, proof he was alive, well, and ready to love again.

Chapter Nineteen

♥

Charlie was as thorough and professional as Madison would have wanted her pilot to be for a small plane hop to L.A. It was a little nerve-racking, but she soon settled in and enjoyed the flight. Especially as Charlie pointed out different places and views that she could connect with. Visualizing the path they were taking on a map helped it all make sense.

Today hadn't started out right, but Caleb had turned things around for her. She had concluded she wasn't supposed to make the flight today, and by extension, leave Dover. It made her question if she was still running away from everything good in her life, trying to chase a dream. Her mother. Joelle. And, of course, Caleb.

Except he'd come to her rescue, and everything was back on track, laying her premise to rest. He had certainly boldly risen to the occasion, surprising her. Including the kiss that left her weak in the knees. The changes in him were remarkable, and Madison couldn't help rejoicing. That she'd been a small part of that change made her feel good, but then there was the part that realized once again they were moving in opposite directions. And this time, she couldn't say he was unavailable...emotionally or otherwise.

"It won't be long now. See, there's the small airstrip where I'm going to land." Charlie pointed to a small tower with an orange wind flag at the top.

Madison swung back around to Charlie. "Oh, I thought we were going to LAX."

The pilot shook his head. "No. It takes a lot more red tape and time to get in there. I try to stick with smaller airports, which end up being quicker overall. Caleb also arranged transportation to pick you up and take you to your interview, and you should be right on time." The older man smiled, his eyes twinkling with merriment.

"That was sweet of him."

Charlie chuckled. "Seems to me he's sweet on you."

Madison could feel the heat suffuse her cheeks. She was unsure how to reply to the comment and remained silent. But it certainly seemed Charlie was right if Caleb's kiss was anything to go by.

Charlie shifted his attention back to the control board and began their descent, communicating with the radio tower.

More and more, Madison had to wonder if she'd been right all along, and that coming to California wasn't what she wanted. People were far more important than jobs.

You designed this right here at our kitchen table. Her mother's words rang in her ears, reminding her of their teary goodbye. Dover didn't need another clothing store, but even on a small scale if she was doing what she loved, and it would put her in the same zip code as the man she loved...wouldn't it be worth it? It was all so confusing.

Charlie landed the plane and true to his word, a driver was there to take her to Sun Glow Fashions. "Thanks for everything. You two must be good friends for you to step up the way you did for me. Have a safe flight home," Madison said, almost sorry to see her new friend leave. He was a connection to Caleb. And Dover. *Home.*

But was it where she belonged?

"Home? I'm not going anywhere just yet. I'll wait for you to finish and fly you back to Texas. No sense in you flying commercial when we're going to the same place. I've got a friend here in town that I'm going to visit for a bit. I'll be back by six and ready to go anytime you are."

Talk about a tremendous relief. A last-minute ticket would have cost her a fortune, and she wasn't sure Sun Glow Fashions would pick up the bill since they would have already been on the hook for her first missed flights. At least they had agreed to still meet with her. "Well, in that case, I won't say no."

Two hours later, she'd left Sun Glow corporate headquarters, dancing with joy in front of the building, holding her hands up to heaven above as she gave thanks to God. Never would she have imagined her interview would go the way it did, especially given her auspicious start to the day. The job was hers. Years of hard work had finally paid off and she was giddy with excitement about what the future might hold.

The entire flight home she had been on cloud nine...literally and figuratively.

It had taken a lot of courage to lay out her plan to the company. Once she realized they still wanted-ed to hire her, she jumped headlong into the idea that had been born from her mother's words. Not only did she get the job, but she would work from home. Remote positions were a big thing nowadays, and the company was all too happy to agree, with a few conditions of their own, of course. A flight to L.A. once a month and her presence at any special corporate affairs was something she had no problem agreeing to, and they had struck a deal.

Madison had a job and could stay in Dover. Talk about having her cake and eating it too. Now if only she could have a double layer of frosting to make it perfect.

She laughed as she exited the taxi and made her way up the sidewalk to her house. Except her mother wasn't home. She must have been picked up by one of her friends for their book club night. Madison dropped her things and grabbed the keys to her car and headed for Caleb's house, grateful she wasn't reliant on her mother's vehicle for transportation anymore. There weren't any promises between them, but his kiss goodbye spoke volumes. Sharing her good news, she would trust her heart to lead the way.

It was time to hang up her running shoes, and hopefully, Caleb would be a part of her life. And if she'd read too much into the kiss, then so be it. No matter what, he was important enough in her life, even as a friend. Love was magical and something to be shared. Either way, Madison would find peace and joy in her own life and for herself, right here in Dover.

Caleb and Joelle would be the frosting on the cake.

Madison pulled into the driveway and was thrilled to catch Caleb just coming in from the barn. Joelle was nowhere in sight, which was odd considering the two were never far apart, not to mention it was late. Maybe she was in bed, and he'd forgotten to do something for Star.

He stopped and waited for her to park. She slid out of the car and headed in his direction, Caleb meeting her halfway. "Hey there. This is a nice surprise. How did it go?" he asked.

Madison found it difficult to contain her elation. She clapped her hands together and laughed. "I was offered the job. Can you believe it?"

"Of course, I do. Who wouldn't want you? Congratulations. You deserve it for all your hard work."

"Thank you," she said, resisting the urge to throw herself into his arms to see where it might lead.

"So, when do you leave for California?"

Madison grinned. This was the best part of her news. "I don't."

"Slow down. I don't follow you because I swear you just said you turned them down."

"Not quite. I said they offered me the job, and that I wasn't moving to California. There is another possibility other than refusing the job."

"Such as?"

Madison gazed up at Caleb, hoping he would see the love in her eyes and understand. "Well, you see... I got to thinking ...a man who kisses me the way you did…doesn't come around often, and well, love is most important. And family. You stepped up to make sure I could go after my dream job. You were there for me. And I want to build a relationship with you and Joelle and be around my mom. This is where I belong. I'm staying in Dover and going to work from home. Other than a few trips to corporate now and then, that is."

Caleb's smile was as bright as the moon shining down on them. "That's wonderful news. Like an answer to my prayers." He pulled her close, wrapping his arms around her.

"I was hoping you would say that." Madison grinned. It would seem her cake came with frosting after all. Her heart raced as he lowered his head closer. She waited, wanting a repeat performance of his kiss at the airport.

He paused. "I have one question, though, and it's pretty important."

"What's that?"

"Next Friday night is the Country Music Festival in Austin." A smile tugged at the corners of his mouth.

"Wow, you are stepping up and out. Nice. By the way, where's Joelle?"

"Staying overnight at her friend's house."

Talk about a huge surprise. "Are you for real? This is such a big change," Madison said, thrilled to see just how much Caleb was embracing life again.

"Someone I care about convinced me life was for living, not hiding."

"Anyone I know?" she asked, pretty sure she knew the answer. Her heart swelled with love for the man standing there...now only if he would kiss her.

Caleb chuckled. "Probably. I'm taking her to the festival Friday night as my date if she'll ever let me ask."

"Is that what you're doing? Asking me on a date?" she teased.

"Seems that way."

Madison decided to take matters into her own hands. "In that case, I accept." She closed the distance between them to kiss Caleb. Warm and inviting. Soft and tender.

Perfect.

Chapter Twenty

♥

Finally, the weekend was just around the corner, and Madison was ready for some downtime. The past week and a half had been a whirlwind of activities. Between getting settled into a new apartment, buying what she needed for the place, and setting up her design office, it had been a non-stop blur.

Caleb was busy at the store. All day, every day...although he found plenty of opportunity to drop by her apartment and lend a hand. Joelle spent time in between the store and with Madison, the two of them having great fun decorating. Not that Joelle could do much, but her efforts were more than a little endearing.

It wouldn't be long before Joelle started kindergarten, so in the meantime she and Caleb made this schedule work. Her mother pitched in often, more than thrilled at the change of events. Not only had her daughter moved home, but it looked as though she might get her wish regarding an expanded family. And then, with the store making money again, Caleb planned on hiring another employee at the store to ease both his and Tommy's schedules.

Her mother was watching Joelle tonight while she and Caleb went to the Country Music Festival. It was silly, but the butterflies in her stomach could only be described as giddy excitement. Which is why she was already getting dressed and there were still two hours before Caleb would pick her up.

Madison had whipped up a special design for the occasion, staying up late to work on the dress. Off the shoulder on one side, it accentuated her waist and flared out to her knees. And all in a dazzling blue chiffon intertwined with a sea green silk, the folds practically floating as she walked. Madison finished getting dressed, styled her hair into long ringlets, and added a touch or two of makeup, using the same colors around her eyes as the dress itself.

She stepped back to examine the finished look in the mirror. Satisfied, she poured a glass of water and sat in one of the front living room chairs to keep a watch out for her date. Waiting made her nervous, but the second she laid eyes on Caleb, her nerves vanished.

Dressed in black jeans, a white dress shirt and bolo tie, and sporting a black long tail jacket, Caleb was mouth-watering gorgeous. Madison was the luckiest woman in the world at that moment and she met him at the door with a smile of approval.

Caleb whistled. "Wowser. You are as beautiful as ever. He stepped closer, holding out a delicate pink corsage before slipping it over her wrist.

"Thank you. You look pretty good yourself." She grinned.

"Shall we?" He offered his arm and escorted her to the truck. Madison scooted over next to him like they were kids on their first date.

The music played from his radio, a sweet country song she had heard a hundred times before, but for the life of her she couldn't name the tune. Her focus was on the man next to her. "Do you like to dance or are you the stand around and listen to the music kind of guy?" she asked when they stopped at the red light.

"It's been years, but I reckon I can figure it out if the right lady asks me to dance," he teased, shooting her a wink.

Madison wasn't sure if his answer was good or bad. Good because she really wanted to dance with Caleb. Bad because she was more nervous now than she had ever been on prom night, a testimony to the very difference in the way she felt about him. "It's been years for me too."

"Then I reckon we will figure it out together or be the laughingstock of the town."

"Well, okay then." She nodded.

Caleb parked the truck and came around to open her door. He took her hand as she slid out. "After you."

"Thank you. I love a gentleman who hasn't forgotten the word chivalry."

"Music to my ears. Your words and the band playing one of my favorite songs." They walked side by side, throngs of people everywhere she looked. Eating. Laughing. Dancing. Playing games. And riding the Ferris wheel. Against the evening sky, the lights of the big wheel stood out, a wave of nostalgia hitting her head on. She hadn't been to the festival since she was in high school, but even then, it hadn't seemed to be filled with such excitement in the air.

Madison suspected her revelation was centered on Caleb.

"Let's stop here and get an Elephant Ear," Caleb suggested.

"Oh, yum. The best one is the plain one with just powdered sugar on it. Lots and lots of powdered sugar. I don't know why people love to overload them with all sorts of crazy toppings."

"So, we'll have to agree to disagree. I knew there had to be something we wouldn't agree on." He chuckled.

Madison frowned. "What do you mean?"

"My favorite is an ear with bananas, chocolate sauce, and whipped cream on the top."

"Yuk. Sounds closer to a banana split than an elephant ear." They moved to stand in line.

"That's because I love banana splits. It's my way of combining my two favorite desserts. Joelle's the one who got me started down this path, so blame her." Caleb chuckled.

Caleb placed their orders. "At least you didn't say chili. Only in Texas would they dream of putting chili on a dessert. Yuk."

"Yuk is right, but I reckon it's more popular in other places than you could possibly imagine. There's so many names for elephant ears, I can't even remember them all. But they are a staple food at every fair in the country."

The man handed them their food and they sat down at one of the empty picnic tables. "What else do you like to do at the festival? I mean aside from eating and dancing."

"Try my hand at some of the skill games, I reckon. Joelle doesn't need any more stuffed animals, but she sure does love adding to her collection. Makes me feel like a winning father when her eyes light up with joy if I knock the milk cans down or sink a basket."

"You are a winning father, whether you win or not." She meant every word and hoped at some point he would see himself the way others saw him. A dedicated dad determined to do right by his daughter.

"Thank you. Seeing as we are about done here..." he stood and tossed the trash into the nearby can. "May I have this dance?" Caleb asked, taking her by the hand.

"Of course, I was wondering when you'd get around to asking." Not that she would dance with anyone else, because all her dances were just for him.

They moved to the dance floor, hand in hand. It was a fast song, and she was pleased to see Caleb was a skilled dancer. None of those crazy chicken moves some boys did because they didn't know any other way. He moved to the groove, all the while smiling and laughing like he was having the time of his life. *An echo of how she felt.*

The music slowed, and he drew her into his arms. "Finally."

They fit together perfectly, and Madison wrapped her arms around his neck, moving in close. She laid her head on his shoulder, wishing this moment would last forever. He tipped her head back and gazed down at her, a smoldering look in his eyes. Caleb lowered his head and kissed her.

A magical kiss in a magical moment. This was the one she wished could last forever.

"Since when do adults go for PDA's?" an elderly woman asked, grinning.

Caleb shot the woman a wink. "When they're on a first date with a woman who has him all tied up in knots." He chuckled.

"Stop it." Madison swatted his arm playfully.

"Got yourself a keeper young lady," the woman said before moving off to join some of her friends.

"What? I feel like the luckiest man in the world when it comes to love. First Lauren, and now you. I think she's smiling down from heaven and would be happy for all of us."

"That's funny because I was thinking the same thing. The part about being the luckiest girl in the world. And I agree, Lauren would approve. I'm in love for the first time in my life."

"And I'm in love for the last time of mine." Caleb dropped another kiss on her mouth before they finished the dance, and he led her off the dance floor. "I'll be right back after I get us some punch. Save me another dance," he added, walking away.

"Always," Madison answered, even if only to herself.

The whole evening was turning out to be one big magical moment made up of smaller, but spectacular moments in time. *Luckily, when the clock struck midnight, she wouldn't have to disappear.*

Caleb's heart was overflowing with love, and it was all because of Madison. And as for Joelle, she had fallen in love with Madison almost from the start. *Smart girl.*

Madison and Joelle chased after the soccer ball while Caleb loaded up the picnic supplies. Horseback riding was quickly becoming a favorite for him again and he loved Joelle's shared passion for all things horses. His daughter was so much like her mother, but now, when Caleb thought of Lauren, he felt a sense of peace. The joy of the memories they shared were to be embraced with love, not anger. Life was made to live...a lesson he was relearning every day being around Madison and Star.

He glanced up at the sky, noting that a few dark clouds had rolled in, and it was probably time to head back to the house. But he wanted them to have as much fun as they could, while they could. The day had started with a fifty percent chance of rain, but thanks to Madison, Caleb now thought of it as a fifty percent chance it *wouldn't* rain. And because of it, they'd set out on this picnic and had hours of fun instead of being stuck inside for rain that might not even happen.

A few sprinkles landed on his arm. "We should probably head back, don't you think?" he asked.

Madison stopped to look up at the sky. "I agree. Those are some heavy-duty rain clouds rolling in this way."

"Aww, but I was having fun," Joelle said.

"There's always more fun at the house. We just need to find it," Caleb said, strapping the bags onto Star's saddle. He held out Sierra's reins to Madison. The new mare got along perfectly with Star and made it so they could ride all the time. Together.

Joelle rode back to the house with him, and by the time they arrived, it was pouring. His soaked shirt clung to his upper body, but he didn't care...not in the slightest. And clearly it didn't bother his daughter either, as she stuck out her tongue, trying to catch the raindrops. Madison's hair hung limply on her shoulders, but she didn't seem to mind one bit.

They tied the horses up in the barn. He would need to come back out in a few minutes to brush them down and feed them, but first, he would take care of the special ladies in his life.

Taking Joelle by the hand, he started running for the house. A huge puddle had filled with the torrential downpour and Caleb started to go around it, but then stopped. An image of when he was a boy came to mind. Puddle jumping was a favorite pastime of his. "Watch this, Joelle." Caleb let go of her hand and ran right through the middle of the puddle, not caring that his boots and jeans were getting wet.

Exhilarating.

"Can I do it too, Daddy?" Joelle asked, her smiling face his first clue this had been an excellent decision.

Caleb nodded. "Of course. We're already wet, so what's the big deal?"

Madison watched them both, a disbelieving expression on her face.

"Come on, Madison. Water's warm," he said, holding out a hand.

"What have you done with Caleb Duncan?" she hollered loud enough to be heard over the downpour.

"He's right here. With you." Caleb tapped his heart.

Madison shook her head and smiled. Seconds later, she took the plunge and joined them as they danced in the rain. "This reminds me of when we met at the park."

"A wonderful day in my life," Caleb said, taking her hand.

"All that's missing is the dog."

"True. Guess we'll have to see what we can do about changing that part."

"Are we getting a dog?" Joelle asked, her eyes bright and shining, and more than making up for the lack of sunshine.

He nodded. "I don't see why not, sweetheart." Caleb pulled Madison in for a hug and kissed her, not caring his daughter was standing there. That's what true love did to you.

"Yay," she squealed, dancing in the puddle until she was soaked from head to toe. "I'm getting a dog and a new mommy. Right, Daddy? You did kiss Madison."

"We'll see, but I'm thinking you might be right." All three of them hugged and laughed in the rain, embracing all the joy that life had brought their way.

Epilogue

Five months later...

Joelle had started kindergarten and loved it, along with her new friends, and especially her new teacher. But most of all, she loved Madison with all her heart. Like father, like daughter. He had talked to Joelle about making Madison a permanent part of the family and she had been thrilled. Of course, getting her to keep quiet until he officially asked Madison to marry him hadn't been easy.

Two weeks later, he had it all planned out right down to the smallest of details...the ring. Joelle helped him pick it out, and he had to admit, his daughter had excellent taste. With the store making money again, life had returned to normal...only better.

His uncle would complete his GA classes and start his golden years over. Caleb had even agreed to let him come to work at the store. After all, he was family, and he knew the store better than anyone. It would be some time, and maybe never, that he would be in charge of anything, but perhaps it was better this way. They were at least on the same page and his uncle held no grudges for the change in his life, and well, Caleb held no grudges for the trouble he'd caused. It was water under the bridge now.

Star had been Caleb's blessing. The day he had set out to rescue Joelle turned out to be the beginning of his rescue. Riding Star and the freedom and joy he found in horseback riding once again had opened his heart to see life. And from there, Madison had been a constant reminder of the good things in life, the parts he wanted to share.

Caleb wished he knew who had sent him Star as a gift, but he had also come to realize it didn't matter.

This was a pay-it-forward legacy.

A tradition Caleb intended to fulfill. Come Spring, he was setting into motion for Star to be bred. Once that happened, he would start his search for the right person who needed hope and healing. Someone who would love the foal and honor the legacy. Someone who needed Sundancer's Joy, the name they had picked out for Star's first foal and the next in line as part of Sundancer's Legacy.

It was a little colder today than he would have liked, but Caleb was eager to put his plan into motion. They were all meeting at the park to let Sergio, the new dog, run around and play. Of course, he could do that at Caleb's place as well, which is why it hadn't been easy for Caleb to get Madison on board, but Joelle had helped on that front. His daughter had worked her charm and convinced Madison she wanted to swing on the playground.

The perfect excuse.

He opened the truck door, and the dog jumped down.

"Sergio, here boy," Madison called out when she spotted them in the parking lot.

The dog took off at full speed, eager to play. Caleb caught up with them, dropping a kiss on Madison's cheek as they watched Joelle play with the dog.

"I'm glad you thought of this. With winter just closing in, there will be less and less days to play outside like this," Madison said, her cheeks tinged with pink from the cold.

Caleb nodded. "That's what I was thinking. This was the perfect opportunity to make a memory."

"Oh," she said, grinning. "What do you have in mind?"

"Joelle, look what I've got," Caleb said, holding up the tennis ball he pulled from his pocket.

"Yay. It's about time." She ran to join them, Sergio leading the way. Except Sergio didn't stop, instead grabbing the ball out of Caleb's hand and making a beeline for the water.

"No, Sergio!" Caleb hollered. "This isn't the time to play fetch in the water." The dog was going to ruin everything. He raced after Sergio, the others following him.

The dog ran into the water, thinking they were playing a game.

Woof. Woof. When he barked, the ball dropped out of his mouth and floated away, the wind pushing it further out of reach.

"Fetch, Sergio," Caleb commanded, hoping for once the dog would do what he was told. They were still working on commands, but so far, the mutt they adopted from the pound wasn't on board. The dog looked at him and then at the ball, unsure what game they were playing.

Caleb watched as the toy drifted about fifteen feet away, not coming closer to shore. "I've got to get that ball."

"We can get him another one," Madison said, coming to stand behind him.

"No, we can't. I need this one." He wasn't willing to offer any more of an explanation because it would ruin his not-so-well-planned surprise. There was only one thing to do...go in after the ball.

"Daddy, what about..."

Caleb shook his head, giving her a silent warning. "Not now, sweetheart. I've got to get the ball."

Sergio came out of the water and shook, spraying all of them. Madison and Joelle screamed with laughter. Caleb was the only one not laughing, but then the thought of the cold pond didn't sound like much fun. The ball continued to drift down the shore, leaving him no choice. Taking off his shoes, he rolled up his pants and tentatively stuck his foot in the water. The cold water was a bit of a shock, but he had little choice in the matter.

All his planning was wiped out, and not once had he considered this as a possibility. He had to get the ball...before it sank. And it would sink, considering the hole he put in it.

Madison chuckled. "Caleb, stop. It's not that important. This isn't like you."

"Someone once told me to roll with the punches when life doesn't go as planned. That's what I'm doing. Only in this case, it's go wading." He moved out a little further, Sergio joining in the game. "Thanks, boy." Caleb started laughing. His proposal was floating away, and everyone thought he'd lost his mind.

But he'd lost his heart.

To Madison.

Just a few more steps and he grabbed the ball, holding it high over his head.

Woof. Woof.

"No, boy. Sorry. Maybe later. After I get warmed up at home," Caleb said. The second he hit the shore, Madison was handing him his socks and shoes, taking the ball from him.

"Thanks. But don't let him have the ball. Please," Caleb insisted. He sat down on the ground, the warmth of his socks a welcome relief.

"What is so important about this ball?" Madison asked, glancing down at it.

Caleb stood and moved to stand next to her. "Joelle, can you hold Sergio for a second?" He snapped the leash on the dog's collar and then handed it to his daughter.

"Finally," Joelle said, her joy resonating as she realized it was time for the surprise.

He took the ball from Madison, then dropped to one knee and held it up to her. "Madison Bradley, I love you with all my heart. Joelle loves you with all her heart. Will you marry me and become a part of our family?"

Tears slipped down Madison's face, and she brushed them away. "I don't understand. You're proposing with a dirty dog ball?"

"No, I am proposing with what's inside the ball. This will always be a special memory for me because it's when you came into our life." He pressed open the small flap of the plastic ball and dropped a ring into his hand and then held it up. "Will you? Marry us?"

"Oh, my goodness." Her eyes glazed over as tears formed and slid down her face. "Yes, yes, yes! I will marry you. I would love to be a part of your forever family. This is where I belong," Madison said, her sunshine smiles all the warmth he would ever need as he slid the ring on her finger.

"Yay!" Joelle danced in circles and hugged Madison.

Sergio barked and danced around everyone.

Caleb kissed his fiancé. "You taught me life is for living, and with you by my side, my heart is full and more than ready to see what adventures life has in store for us. I love you."

"I love you, too. Both of you. My forever family."

***

If you enjoyed this sweet and charming romance, be sure to watch for the Sundancer's Legacy
releases throughout 2024, and check out the ALSO BY ELSIE DAVIS section on the next page for more clean and wholesome romance!

BONUS READ

Want to keep in touch with new releases and what's happening in the world of Elsie Davis? Sign up for the monthly newsletter at Elsie Davis HEA (Happily-Ever-After) and enjoy DIGGING THE DRIVER (A Celebrity Corgi Romance) as a FREE BOOK!

The greatest compliment you could give an author is to leave a review in order to help other readers discover the same great stories you enjoyed. Amazon/Bookbub/Goodreads are all great places. Many thanks!!!
Another great way to keep in touch - ***Follow Elsie Davis on FaceBook***

Also By Elsie Davis

Sweet, Clean and Wholesome Stories...with a Happily-Ever-After Guarantee!

Holidays in Hallbrook
(Sweet Romance Series for Holidays Throughout the Year)
Welcome to Hallbrook, New Hampshire. A small-town filled with the unexpected, lots of love, and of course, a beloved dog to ramp up the excitement.
Love & Order (Labor Day)
Love & Family (Thanksgiving)
Love & Peace (Christmas)
Love & Chocolate (Valentine's Day)
Love & Hope (Mother's Day)

Love & Liberty (Independence Day)
Love & Honor (Veteran's Day)
Love & Joy (Easter)
Love & Adventure (Father's Day)

Great Smoky Mountain Getaways
(Christian Inspirational – Women's Fiction Romances)
Juliet's Journey to Love
Poppy's Path to Love
Rachel's Road to Love
Taylor's Trek to Love – Spring 2024

Crossroads Creek Cowboys
(Christian Inspirational Romances)
The Heart of a Cowboy
The Help of a Cowboy
The Return of a Cowboy
The Care of a Cowboy

Crestfield Inn Romances

If you like special kinds of soulmates, a splash of the supernatural, and wholesome relationships, you'll adore this sweet bit of fun filled with romance and mystery.

Turning Back Time
Turning Up Roses
Turning Down Pie

Celebrity Corgi Romance
(Standalone Sweet Romance)
If you like light mystery mixed in with your happily-ever-after, you'll enjoy this second-chance romance and the race to save an adorable Corgi.
Digging the Driver

Gold Coast Retrievers
(Sweet Romance)
Special Golden Retrievers help their humans solve mysteries, save lives, and even find love...
Defending Dakota

Trinity River
(Sweet Western Romance)
Ranchers and farmers depend on the Trinity River for water, but when a secret conglomerate starts buying up property by fair means or foul, it's time for the landowners of Tumble County to fight back—Texas style. But what they don't count on, is finding love in the process.
Back in the Rancher's Arms
Small Town, Big Secrets

Sundancer's Legacy – 9 Book series

Sundancer's Star

Coming Soon – 2024
Sundancer's Joy
Sundancer's Heart
Sundancer's Majesty
Sundancer's Miracle

Sundancer's Glory
Sundancer's Kiss
Sundancer's Moon
Sundancer's Splendor

About The Author

Elsie Davis is a *USA Today and International Best-selling Author* of over 25 sweet, clean, and wholesome romances, and a member of the ACFW. She discovered the world of Happily-Ever-After romance at the age of twelve when she began avidly reading Barbara Cartland, the Queen of Romance, and has been hooked ever since. After building her dream log home on top of a small mountain, she turned her attention to do what she loves most, writing. Elsie writes sweet Contemporary Romance and Contemporary Christian Romance from her heart...hoping to share a little love in a big world.

When she's not writing, she can be found birding, kayaking, camping, fishing, playing disc golf, and taking nature walks—hoping to spot wildlife. Basically, she loves all things outdoors, EXCEPT cold weather. She and her husband are avid Caribbean cruisers, but Elsie's favorite vacation was their cruise to Alaska. (In spite of the cold!) Indoors, she enjoys a toasty fire, and of course, a great romance with a guaranteed Happily-Ever-After.

https://www.elsiedavishea.com